Courage in Korea

COURAGE IN KOREA

Stories of the Korean War

Selected by

Albert B. Tibbets

BOSTON LITTLE, BROWN AND COMPANY TORONTO

*Published simultaneously in Canada
by Little, Brown & Company (Canada) Limited*

PRINTED IN THE UNITED STATES OF AMERICA

ACKNOWLEDGMENTS

For permission to reprint copyrighted material the following acknowledg-
ments are gratefully made:

To Curtis Brown, Ltd. for "Caught Between the Lines" by William
Douglas Lansford, © 1959 by The Curtis Publishing Company. Reprinted
from the *Saturday Evening Post* by permission of the author.

To William Morris Agency, Inc. for "The Wrong Way to Win a War" by
John Godey, copyright 1953 by The Crowell-Collier Publishing Company.
Reprinted from *Collier's* by permission of William Morris Agency, Inc.

To Littauer and Wilkinson for "Trial by Combat" by William Chamberlain, copyright 1951 by The Curtis Publishing Company. Reprinted from
the *Saturday Evening Post* by permission of Littauer and Wilkinson. And
for "The Enemy Beach" by William Chamberlain, copyright 1950 by The
Curtis Publishing Company. Reprinted from the *Saturday Evening Post* by

ACKNOWLEDGMENTS *(continued)*

permission of Littauer and Wilkinson. And for "The Chaplain of Company C" by William Chamberlain, copyright 1951 by The Curtis Publishing Company. Reprinted from the *Saturday Evening Post* by permission of Littauer and Wilkinson. And for "Heroes Don't Sound Off" by William Chamberlain, copyright 1958 by The Curtis Publishing Company. Reprinted from the *Saturday Evening Post* by permission of Littauer and Wilkinson. And for "General from the Pentagon" by Francis Chase, Jr., copyright 1953, by The Curtis Publishing Company.

To Brandt and Brandt for "The Bloodstained Beach" by Jacland Marmur, copyright 1952 by The Curtis Publishing Company. First published in the *Saturday Evening Post,* by permission of Brandt and Brandt.

To Emile C. Schurmacher for "Spy Mission to Inchon," copyright 1957 by Magazine Management Company. Reprinted from *Stag Magazine* by permission of the author. And for "Sky Over Pyongyang," copyright 1953 by the MacFadden Publications. Reprinted from *Saga* by permission of the author.

To friends of many years in Scouting,
Boy Scouts of America:

Dr. Elbert K. Fretwell
Chief Scout and former Chief Scout Executive

Joseph A. Brinton, Jr.
Chief Scout Executive

Joseph H. Brinton
Scout Executive Detroit Area Council 262

Contents

"No Farther," Said the Young Men

INCHON, Pusan, Sinuiju, Taebu-do, Chinnampo — when the call for help came from the United Nations to join in defending South Korea, these names were only dots on the map of Asia to the young men of Maine and Florida, of Texas and California, of Montana and Nebraska and all the states in between.

The call went out because South Korea was threatened by the Communists, invading from the North contrary to an agreement with Russia. And the United Nations had promised to stand by the South Koreans in their determination to have an independent and democratic government. So the United States, as a member of the United Nations, sent our American young men to the defense of the gallant little nation. On troopships and minesweepers, in submarines and planes, they crossed the Pacific Ocean.

There, in foxholes, in burnt-out splotches of rice paddies where straw-thatched houses squatted in the rain, on shores where gumbo mud was waist-deep and where the heat fell over the water like a hot blanket, our men took their firm stand against the invaders. The ships they manned kept open the Yellow Sea and the Korean Sea, and the water lanes of the ocean. The planes they flew freed the air.

As they stopped the Communist advance with fierce fighting, our men came to know the gentle Korean men and women and children. They felt these friends' bewilderment that their simple way of living was threatened. And their determination deepened that the land of South Korea must be kept for its people. It must remain theirs.

In the stories in this book, you will be with our young men as they made their gallant, unyielding stand in that distant land. You will share in their courage and their comradeship. And you will understand what it meant in hardship and suffering for them to say to the Communists: *"No Farther."*

COURAGE IN KOREA

Trial by Combat

by William Chamberlain

HE WAS two months past twenty and looked younger, and he sat in a foxhole above a little Korean town while he wrote a letter to his girl back in the States. An empty ration carton served as a desk for the single dirty sheet of paper which was all that he had left. It was bitter cold and his fingers stiffened as he wrote.

Presently he stopped for a moment, putting the stub of pencil carefully down on the frozen ground beside him and thrusting his hand beneath his parka to warm his fingers while he stared at the bleak, snow-covered landscape in front. Here and there he could see other holes where the rest of his platoon lay. It was the first platoon of Baker Company and it had been out here on the hill for three days now and, the way things looked, it was liable to be out here for a long while longer. If the gooks didn't gobble it up, that is.

The boy's name was John Moulton, but he had been known as "Mike" back in the school in Georgia which he had left just five weeks ago now. He was a second lieutenant of infantry — an expendable item — and he had commanded the first platoon of Baker Company for ten days. The gold of his bars was still so bright that it would have lighted up the gray afternoon if he had been wearing bars. He wasn't. He was wearing muddy battle clothes and the only bright item about him was the carbine leaning close to his hand.

The veterans of Baker Company had been watching him out of the corners of their eyes since he had joined the division. They were tough men who had been tempered in the bitter fighting on the Pusan perimeter and honed bright in the pursuit up to Pyongyang. They didn't think much of green-kid shavetails. Particularly not now that the enemy had turned, snarling and dangerous, and was pouring it on again. They still remembered Lieutenant Jablonski — now there was a platoon leader for you, bud! Only, Lieutenant Jablonski had taken a bullet through his belly at Huyong and had been evacuated to the States.

Sergeant Murphy put the thing into words as he squatted in a foxhole with the BAR team of his squad. Sergeant Murphy had been with the division for a long time and he took a dim view of kid lieutenants who didn't even shave regularly. Not that you did much shaving in a freezing foxhole on a hill in Korea.

"This outfit has been snafued ever since it came to this condemned island," he said gloomily. "Now they give us this baby lootenant an' we're really snafued. We're double-snafued."

Private Dowdy, assistant BAR man, looked up and shook his head. He was slight and pinch-faced and he had been a schoolteacher before he had joined the Army. He had a passion for accuracy.

"This isn't an island, Sergeant," he said reproachfully. "You're always calling it an island. It's a peninsula."

Murphy grunted sourly. He had a boil starting on the back of his neck and the thought of it made him unhappy.

"Island. Peninsula. Continent. I don't give a hoot

what it is, sonny. All I know is that I don't like it. I don't like bein' snafued, either."

Corporal Grosbeck, the BAR man, beat his arms to start the circulation.

"Quit beefing," he said. "Don't you know that the infantry is always snafued? The only difference is that sometimes they're plain snafued and other times they're blank snafued."

"What's blank snafued?" Murphy asked suspiciously.

"My mother don't like me to use that kind of language," Corporal Grosbeck said piously. "The gooks have been awful quiet today. You suppose they're up to some of their nasty little tricks?"

"They're always up to nasty little tricks," Murphy said sourly.

He sighed gustily and stared across the shallow valley to where other hills made a dun rampart against the sky. There were gooks in those hills, he thought. Chinks, too, probably. In the middle of the valley a small river made a dark ribbon.

Dowdy was frowning thoughtfully. "It doesn't make sense to call a peninsula an island," he said. "An island is a —"

"Forget it," Murphy said crossly. He was acutely aware of that impending boil. It hadn't begun to hurt much yet, but he knew that it would. "What do I care what an island is? I got enough trouble."

"Somebody's coming through the brush," Corporal Grosbeck said.

Murphy reached for his rifle, calling "Who's there?" in a brittle voice.

"Oleson," somebody answered from up the hill, and the three men in the foxhole relaxed again.

"Well, come on in out of the rain!" Murphy called. "We movin' back for a rest?" he added hopefully.

Oleson, one of the platoon messengers, slithered through the brush and dropped down into the hole. "Naw," he said, blinking his pale eyes. "We ain't moving back."

"What you doin' up here in the front line, then? Buckin' for a medal?"

"What do you mean 'front line'?" Oleson wanted to know angrily. "You know darn well I been squatting in a hole not thirty yards up the hill all the time! The lieutenant wants to see you."

"What's he want to see me about?"

"We're going on a patrol across the river tonight," Oleson told him.

"Snafued," Murphy said sadly, "double-snafued. Maybe triple-snafued."

"Blank snafued," Corporal Grosbeck agreed.

Mike picked up his stub of pencil again. *I am sitting in a hole on a hill somewhere in Korea,* he wrote. *It is quite cold here and there is quite a little snow.*

He paused for a moment, wetting the point of the pencil with his tongue while he stared across the bleak landscape and tried to think of what to write next. He couldn't keep his mind on the letter very well because he was thinking of the platoon. It was his platoon and he had to look out for it. The fear that he might somehow let it down was a little mouse-gnaw of worry which was constantly with him.

His mind kept going over the things that they had taught him a platoon leader should do. The book was specific about such things and they had seemed simple enough in the classroom back at Fort Benning. They looked different when you were out in a fox-hole, though, with the gooks across the river. Then, too, the cautious reserve of the men in the platoon worried him. They were strangers and he could sense their distrust. He hadn't exactly counted on that, he thought.

He thought back, a little regretfully, to the two years that he had spent as a soldier before they had sent him to Officer Candidate School and then pinned the gold bars on his shoulders. He remembered the evenings in barracks with the roistering crapshooters busy at one end and big Ed Henderson lying on his bunk with his arms behind his head while he regaled them with outrageous lies. He could even remember with a little pleasure the comradeship of sitting in a bucket seat of the big transport, hands clasped across his emergency chute to hold down the emptiness in his belly while he waited for the jump master to sing out hoarsely, "Okay, you troopers! Stand up and hook up!"

Oleson, one of his messengers, broke into his thoughts. "The cap'n wants to talk to you, sir."

Oleson passed across the radiophone, and Mike pushed the button and said, "Moulton, sir," and then listened while the company commander's voice came in little crackles out of the receiver. As he listened he made little scribbles on his message pad: ". . . Hill 201 . . . move out at 1800 . . . stay in observation until tomorrow night . . . artillery support on call . . . sending you a battalion aid man." The crackles died away, and Mike said, "Yes, sir," and handed the radio back to Oleson, who scowled dourly at the instrument.

"We goin' on another patrol?" he asked without enthusiasm.

Mike nodded absently. "Yeah," he said. He had started to say, "What did you think we were going to do, bud? Go fishing?" That was what he would have said if he had still been a sergeant — one of the gang. Well, he wasn't. Instead, he added, "Get Sergeant Danton and tell the squad leaders to report here in ten minutes."

Oleson said, "Yes, sir," in a noncommittal voice and crawled on out across the lip of the foxhole.

Mike watched until he had disappeared, and then picked up the stub of pencil again.

I sure do miss you, he wrote. *Don't worry about me, though, honey. It's mearly a question of time before I'll be back.* He stopped writing and scowled at the "mearly" — it didn't look right. He never had been able to spell. He scratched the word out and wrote "only" instead, and slipped the unsealed letter into his pocket.

The platoon sergeant, Danton, came sliding down into the hole. He was a slender man, ten years older than Mike, with bright hard eyes and an air of competent arrogance about him. He had got a Silver Star in the Pusan fighting and had been acting platoon leader before Mike had arrived to take over. Danton had resented that.

"You want to see me?" he asked.

Mike nodded. "We've got orders to cross the river tonight," he said. "It could be a rough deal."

"I've seen rough deals," Danton said, and Mike could feel his face reddening. Danton's lazy tone was saying: "Scared, huh?"

"I've sent for the squad leaders," Mike heard himself saying. "We'll wait until they get here; then I'll give you your orders. Save time that way."

Why was he explaining his actions to Danton? The man had sense enough to know that you gave orders that way. It was almost as though he was apologizing to the man for something. Danton's smile showed that he thought that too.

After a moment, Sergeant Murphy came through the brush, and then Ladd and Epstein — squad leaders of the other two squads — joined him. Mike looked at each of them as he cleared his voice a little uncertainly.

"We've got orders to cross the river at 1800 tonight," he began. "We're to get on Hill 201 in order to . . ."

He went on from there with a swift decisiveness.

When he had finished, the four sergeants watched with expressionless faces while he checked back in his mind to see if he had overlooked anything. He hadn't.

"Any questions?" he asked then.

"I don't think your plan will work, Lieutenant," Danton said bluntly.

Well, it had come out now, Mike thought. He was glad, in a way, and his spine stiffened as he looked steadily at his platoon sergeant. "Why not, Danton?"

"The lieutenant is trying to do it by the book," Danton said softly. "Only the book don't work out here. You see, the gooks haven't read the book."

"How would you do it, Sergeant?"

"Spread out more and let each squad go up on its own. That's the way we used to do it when Lieutenant Jablonski was in command."

Mike rubbed a hand across his chin and stared at Hill 201, then shook his head. "No good. Our job is to get on top that hill as quick as we can and all together. A column is the best way to do it. Jablonski's not in command now. The orders stand."

He saw anger spark the backs of Danton's eyes; thought that the man was going to say more, but Danton clamped his lips tight and said nothing.

"If there's no more questions, that's all," Mike told them then, and the four nodded and went on back into the brush.

Oleson came back to slide into the foxhole, but Mike paid no attention; reached, instead, for his carbine and began to rub at the already immaculate action. That little gnaw of worry was sharper now. He wondered if he had done the right thing. Maybe, if Lieutenant Jablonski would have done it differently, he should . . . He let that thought go, jerking his shoulders impatiently. Memory of a thing that his father had once said to him reassured him a little. "Making your own decisions is a part of the loneliness of command, son," the old man had said. "You can't fight wars with committees — not on the front line."

"Check through to battalion," Mike said abruptly to Oleson. "See if that aid man is on his way up."

Twenty yards down the slope, Danton paused beside Sergeant Murphy before angling off to his own foxhole. "Well, here we go, Murph," he said angrily. "That wet-eared shavetail will wash this outfit up like you'd wash a pair of socks. Where you want your Purple Heart sent?"

"Don't ride the kid," Murphy murmured, and was

a little surprised at his own words. "He's got to learn."

Danton spat and allowed his eyes to slide bleakly over Murphy. "Not at the expense of my hide, he don't," he said.

"What you talkin' about, Dan?"

"Figure it out for yourself," Danton said curtly, and swung away into the brush.

Dowdy was talking with Corporal Grosbeck as Murphy came back to the hole. "Now you take mathematics," Dowdy was saying earnestly. "If it wasn't for mathematics, do you think that we'd know anything about the universe or the solar system?"

"I don't know anything about 'em anyway," Grosbeck said.

"I mean people like Einstein — that sort of people. Because they're great mathematicians they can figure anything out."

"I wish they'd figure out a way to get me out of Korea," Grosbeck told him. "That'd be enough for me. . . . What's the scoop, Murph?" he asked as Murphy slid down beside him.

Sergeant Murphy told him, and Grosbeck shook his head sadly. "I should have gone in the Navy," he said.

The winter darkness came down swiftly, bringing snow flurries with it. The battalion aid man had come up at about 1400 — a wispy soldier named Hawkins. Mike had remembered him vaguely from Fort Bragg; remembered that they had drunk beer together on a couple of occasions, and the memory sent a little thread of warmth through him. It was almost as though he had met an old dear friend up here in the hills.

He had said, "Hello, Soldier. Come up to see the war?" and Hawkins had grinned and answered, "Hi, Mike. When'd they let you out of kindergarten?" and then he had flushed and stammered a little as he had added hastily, "I mean 'Lieutenant.' "

"The 'Mike' was good enough," Mike had told him. "Forget the 'Lieutenant' business for a little. We all bleed the same color up here."

That had been all, and Hawkins had moved away to find a hole for himself. His going left Mike more lonely than ever. Eighteen hundred hours seemed a long while in coming, he thought. He wished that time would hurry because, once they had started, that little thread of worry would disappear. At least he hoped it would. . . .

They moved out in a column finally, Mike at its

head with Sergeant Murphy and the first squad, and Sergeant Danton bringing up the rear as they edged cautiously down the slope. They hadn't sighted any gooks on this side of the river so far, but you could never tell. Snow was coming down harder now — light, feathery stuff which clung to the faces of the men.

It took a half-hour to reach the river, and Mike, working forward with Sergeant Murphy, found that the crossing was unguarded. That was good luck. The river was fordable here, Mike knew — he had reconnoitered it when the platoon had first taken its position on the hill three days ago. Water mid-hip-deep and not too swift. He squatted there on his heels, carbine balanced on his knee, while he whispered to Murphy.

"Bring your squad on, Murph," he said, using Murphy's nickname for the first time. "Pass the word back for the rest to wait."

For a moment Sergeant Murphy rested on one knee there in the snow without saying anything. A certain surprise and ease was beginning to grow in him. It had begun back there on the hill when the kid shavetail had cracked down on Danton, and it had been getting stronger since. The way that Mike had brought them up to the river was right and good, and "Murph" was the way he liked it. That was the way that things had been when Lieutenant Jablonski had been in command.

Then he said, "Yes, sir," and faded into the swirling snow; came back presently with his squad ghostly behind him.

The thin ice which edged the river crackled sharply as Mike broke through it, and the bite of the freezing water drove a million needles into his legs. Then he was across, with Murphy and his squad behind him, and still there was no spatter of gook fire. He began to hope that they might reach Hill 201 without a fight. Murphy's squad spread out in a shallow semicircle and Mike called softly back for the two other squads to come on. He waited by the ford until he saw Danton's slender shape come through the drifting snow.

"All across?" Mike asked.

"That's right," Danton said shortly.

"Okay, we'll go on. Keep them closed up."

They went on across the flat of the valley like gray wraiths and then the ground began to rise and Mike knew that they had reached the foot of the hills; hoped that he had hit Hill 201. Mike thought:

These hills all look alike at night and in the snow. He halted the column for a short breather before they started up. It was just past midnight when they came out on the hill's top.

Daylight came slowly with a sullen lightening of the eastern sky as Mike lay in the shallow hole that he had scooped out, but he grinned a little as he put down his field glasses. They were shot with luck, he thought. Dug in on their objective and no sign of gooks yet. A dozen yards to the left, Sergeant Danton lay in a similar hole, and the rest of the platoon was disposed in a tight perimeter on the cone-shaped hill. Mike's eyes felt heavy and tired as he reached for the radiophone.

Baker Company CP came in and he talked for a moment with Harris, the exec. "Nothing to see up here," he said. "How long do we stay here, Pete?"

"I don't know," Harris said in a worried voice. "We're pulling back. I guess you stay until we get clear. If the gooks show up, let us know, kid."

"If any gooks show up, you'll hear me yelling for artillery support clear back to Pyongyang," Mike said, trying to make his voice sound light. He didn't feel light. A cold hand had him by the stomach — it was no fun to be left behind. He said, "So long, Pete."

The gray morning wore on with an unnatural quietness. The snow had stopped for a little while, and its white blanket, which stretched in front of Mike's foxhole, spelled out a temporary and uneasy peacefulness. Oleson slept with a blanket wrapped around him and his mouth making faintly sighing noises. Mike looked at him for a moment, fighting off his own drowsiness, and then fished the unfinished letter from his pocket. Writing would help him to keep awake, he thought.

He wrote: *We are on top of another hill now. It is something like those hills we used to climb in Aurora — not very much like them, though. It snowed some last night.*

He stopped there and put the letter away again. Couldn't keep his mind on what he was writing. There wasn't anything to write about, anyway. After a moment, he took off his boots and rubbed his feet briskly and then pulled his wet socks back on again. The morning dragged on, and at eleven hundred he awoke Oleson and then started out on his round of the other foxholes.

Sergeant Danton was squatting in his shallow hole with his blanket over his shoulders and Hawkins, the aid man, squatted beside him.

"Baby lieutenants!" Danton said bitterly. "Rotten green and scared of their own shadow, and we've got to trust our lives to them! Maybe you like it! I don't!"

Hawkins grunted and stared mildly back at Danton. "You talkin' about Mike, Sarge?"

"That's who I'm talking about."

Hawkins scrubbed absently at the bristles on his cheeks. "Uh-huh. You ever jump out of an airplane, Sarge?"

"What would I want to jump out of an airplane for?"

"Just wondered, is all. It takes guts. Now you take Mike — he's jumped out of airplanes thirty, forty times."

"What do you know about it?"

"I soldiered with him down at Bragg. He was a sergeant then. Busted his ankle once, but he went up and jumped again as soon as they let him out of the hospital. Yeah, takes guts, I guess."

Danton stared dourly back, but didn't answer. Then Mike came crawling through the snow to squat by the foxhole. "Things are too quiet," he said softly to Danton. "I've got a feeling that all hell is going to bust loose pretty quick. What do you think?"

"I think we'd better get out of here," Danton told him curtly. "Get back across the river while we can."

Mike shook his head. "The exec says the outfit is pulling back. We've got to cover them until they get clear."

"Why is it that it's this platoon that's always picked for the dirty jobs?" Danton asked in a harsh voice. "It wasn't that way when Lieutenant Jablonski was in command. He saw to that."

"You're paid to do dirty jobs, Danton," Mike said, and let it go at that. Danton watched him as he went on to the next foxhole. Against his will, Danton was thinking that forty jumps was a lot of jumps. He had always had a fear of airplanes. . . .

It was two o'clock in the afternoon when the attack came. One minute the hills lay empty and peaceful under the snow. The next they were full of yelling, screaming madmen garbed in white, who came bounding in from three sides. Chinese, Mike thought; not gooks. He reached for the radio as he heard Grosbeck's BAR start to hammer with its deliberate rhythm. The whole perimeter rocked with fire as he spoke cryptic words into the transmitter which would bring down artillery fire into the ravine in front.

Oleson's rifle was barking steadily from the lip of the foxhole as Mike reached for his own carbine. The world seemed to be full of white-robed figures which blew bugles and danced crazily as they seemed to sprout out of the snowy ground. Bullets from the perimeter sped toward them and found them, and they went down, but more kept coming.

Between shots Mike thought, This can't last. . . . But it did.

Then a cracking explosion sent a pillar of black smoke up from the far side of the ravine, and Mike knew that the howitzers had joined in the fight. Those blossoming shellbursts looked like money from home. They made a pockmarked pattern against the snow and their echoes rolled back against the hills in a confusion of noise. This, then, was what war was like, Mike thought at the back of his mind. Not much different from what he had expected, except for those bugles. He hadn't counted on them.

A bullet whispered its song close to his head and he crouched lower and placed his shots carefully into those ghosts trying to come up the hill. Then, all at once, the ghosts were gone and the slope was empty and silence fell eerily over the perimeter, except for the crump of the artillery shells still dropping in the ravine. Mike reached for the radio; told the CP to hold the artillery fire. Oleson was looking at him with a white, pinched face.

"I got it, Lieutenant," he said.

Through the shoulder, Mike found, and not too bad. "Lie easy," he told Oleson. "I'll send the aid man in a minute."

He crawled out of the hole and moved to the left. Danton was wiping the bolt of his rifle as Mike came up. "Take care of Oleson," he said to Hawkins, and then spoke softly to the platoon sergeant: "Take over until I get back, Sergeant."

Danton nodded and Mike went on.

He came last to Sergeant Murphy's squad. Murphy lay with his head cradled on his arm as though he slept, and Grosbeck's eyes were bitter as he looked at Mike.

"Curse them!" he said. "They're going to pay for Murph! They're going to pay plenty!"

Mike nodded and placed an arm on Grosbeck's shoulder for a moment. "I know. Take it easy, Soldier," he said.

He didn't realize it, but he had suddenly become vastly older than Corporal Grosbeck; older than any man in the platoon. That was the price that a man paid for a pair of gold bars on his shoulders. He said, "We'll all pay on Murph's account with the gooks before we're through with them."

He went on back to the CP with Grosbeck's eyes following him as the eyes of the other men had followed him as he left their foxholes.

"Not a bad guy," Grosbeck said under his breath to Dowdy. "Not a bad guy at all."

Back in his hole, Mike pushed the button of the transmitter; waited for the company CP to come in. His voice was detached, even as he made his report: one dead; three wounded, not too bad.

The CO's voice, a little worried, came back at him through the gray afternoon. "Can you hold on for a while longer, Moulton?"

"Sure," Mike said. There was nothing else to say.

It was an hour later when the bugles shrilled in the dying day again and the white ghosts bowled up the slopes once more. Again the artillery fires made little red blossoms along the hillsides. The nightmare lasted longer this time, and when it was finished the slope was dotted with ugly little heaps. But the platoon had paid, too — paid more than it could afford. Dietrick gone in the first squad; Malley and

Hines in the second; Warren in the third. Seven more men wounded. Mike felt tired and old as he picked up the transmitter.

"Hang on somehow," the exec told him. He, too, sounded tired. He asked again, "Can do, Mike?"

"Can do," Mike told him automatically.

Darkness came down with the swiftness of a curtain pulled across a stage, and the worry quickened in Mike as he saw it come. The Chinks liked the dark. Well, it couldn't be helped.

Hawkins crawled over to the hole where Sergeant Danton was hunched. In the half-light that remained Hawkins noticed that Danton's eyes seemed to have retreated far back into his head and that his fingers shook as he reached for a cigarette. It wasn't good — Hawkins had seen men act like that before.

"He's crazy!" Danton said violently. "That lieutenant! Why don't we pull back? He'll get us all killed, I tell you!"

"Take it easy," Hawkins said. "Mike will —"

He didn't finish, because the bugles had suddenly started their bawling again — coming from the direction of the river now. A cold moon was lifting above the ragged hills, and shadowy figures raced across the snow in its pale light. Danton turned his head to look;

then swung back and pulled the blanket over his head. He was through. . . .

They threw the Chinese back twice more before midnight, but after each assault the perimeter grew smaller, pulling in on itself as the casualties mounted. Hawkins was busy now — too busy.

He tied up Mike's hand where a grenade splinter had chopped it.

"I used to think that Fort Bragg was the outhouse of creation," he said. "But I wish I was back there right now."

"How bad off are we, Hawkins?"

"Pretty bad. Eleven wounded now. Two pretty bad."

Oleson said slowly to Mike, "The cap'n wants you, sir."

The radiophone crackled. "Pull back across the river, Mike," it said. "The artillery will cover you. Can you move right away?"

"Yes, sir," Mike told him.

No use to say that they were surrounded and cut off — nothing that the CO could do about that now. It was up to the first platoon. Mike nodded at Oleson. "We're pulling back. Pass the word."

"Danton's bad off," Hawkins said. "I've seen 'em go

that way before. It's the tough ones that crack wide
open when they break."

"I'll have a look," Mike told him, and slipped across
to where the platoon sergeant was still huddled in his
blanket. He stared straight with eyes that saw nothing
as Mike shook him by the shoulder. "Get on your
feet, Soldier. We're going back."

"No," Danton said in a dull, old man's voice.

"Help me get him on his feet," Mike said. "Nobody
stays behind. We'll carry him if we have to."

The night was quiet as Mike assembled what was
left of the platoon in the sparse shelter of the scrub.
He made his dispositions hastily — a man to help each
of the wounded who were too badly hurt to fight.
Two men to be carried. He took Oleson and Hawkins
and Danton with him at the head of the column; Sergeant Ladd would bring up the rear with the second
squad.

Artillery fire began to fall in the ravine again as he
said curtly, "Keep closed up. Let's go." They wound
slowly on down the hill, a thin little file of men.

The bugles began their taunt again and fire blossomed along the bordering ridges. Behind them the
sound of their own artillery was a comforting roar.

Somehow — Mike didn't know how exactly — they fought their way back to the river. He spread Ladd's squad out in a shallow semicircle and started the two other squads across. As they went, he could hear bullets hitting the water with nasty little *whick's*.

Epstein called from the far bank that they were across, and Mike waved Sergeant Ladd on up — waited by the water's edge to count the men as they passed.

Sergeant Danton, who had been following Mike like a man walking in his sleep, suddenly lifted his head.

"I'll show the bloody bandits!" he said in a thick voice.

He lifted his rifle and suddenly began to run back across, the way that they had come, his lean shape dodging through the shadows. Ladd's squad was halfway across, but Ladd halted them and started back.

Mike waved him on. "Go on! Get across! I'll take care of Danton!"

Hawkins came splashing back. "Mike you can't —"

"I said to go on!"

"Naw," Hawkins said.

They found Danton curled around a boulder. Blood smeared his face, but his eyes were sane now; spiteful as they looked back at Mike.

"Had to be a hero, did you?" Danton said between his teeth. "Had to do it according to the book. Kid stuff! Why didn't you leave me?"

"This outfit leaves nobody," Mike said. . . . "Give me a hand, Hawkins."

It seemed as if it took a long time to reach the river, but finally Mike felt the icy bite of the water on his legs, and then they were across and the artillery was laying a curtain of fire on the bank they had left. The thin column went on, plodding in the moonlight, and after a while their own hill was in front of them and a squad of the second platoon was there to give them a helping hand.

Mike sat with his back against the ruined wall of a house and took the soiled envelope from his pocket. He dampened the stub of pencil and wrote: *We had a little fight day before yesterday, but don't worry. Everything will be all right.*

There were voices around the corner of the wall, and he paused for a moment to listen idly. It was Sergeant Danton talking to the half-dozen replacements who had come up that morning.

"You've joined a good platoon," Sergeant Danton was saying, "and you've got the best darned platoon leader in the Army. When the Old Man talks to you later this morning, I want you to stand up and look like soldiers."

"Who's the Old Man, Sarge?" a voice wanted to know.

"Lieutenant Moulton to you, bud. Maybe, if you learn to be a soldier, you can call him 'Mike' someday."

Mike felt good all at once — the loneliness was gone now. He moistened the pencil again and added, *This is a swell outfit that I've got. I wish you could see it. Much love, Mike,* and sealed the envelope and put it back in his pocket.

Caught
between the Lines

by W. Douglas Lansford

I WON'T LIE and say I liked or disliked him at first sight. The fact is I thought him a rather funny-looking, not-too-sharp kid. Not that his fatigues weren't creased and his paratrooper boots shined as though he'd just come off parade, instead of up from a battalion headquarters on the Korean front lines.

He was about twenty-five, I'd have guessed. But I didn't have to guess at whether or not he had ears. What he had were two round pink radar antennae sticking out from the sides of a freckled baby face. The fact that he didn't smile, that his brown hair was crew-cut, showing his head to be almost a perfect cantaloupe, and that his eyes were tiny and as serious as a Chihuahua challenging a Saint Bernard, didn't help things one little bit. And then he spoke — and that really did it!

"Sergeant," he squeaked in a voice that sounded as though it were still in the process of changing, "I'm Lieutenant George Poole. Get somebody to unload my gear, and show me where the CO hangs out."

He was standing, legs spread, hands on hips, his steel helmet hanging on his canteen, which in turn was attached to a web belt on which also hung a service forty-five and a regulation carbine bayonet knife. I'd be crowding it to say he was five feet five, but his manner was easily something over eight feet ten — and no mistake.

I looked down at him and nodded. "Okay, sir! Follow me!"

"My gear," he said. "Let's not forget my gear. And if you rugged front-line types can't salute, let's at least show you can still approximate an attention — shall we?"

I found out some interesting facts about Lieutenant George Poole just as soon as I could shake him at the command dugout. The guy who'd driven his jeep up had picked him up at a hospital unit some three miles behind the lines, where the polished little runt had been an officer of the guard. That added, but it was just our unit's luck. He was being assigned to us as the new platoon commander.

"Is he going to hold full-dress parade every morning, Sergeant?" asked Hoop Keeler sourly.

Hoop was a big, lazy Oklahoman, and about the best squad leader I had.

"I'm not a mind reader," I told him. "Get back to your job."

When he shot a fast glance over my shoulder and then batted up the hill, I did a little mind reading after all and turned around. Sure enough, our new Napoleon was walking toward me. Then I did a double-take and almost passed out. He had a swagger stick under his arm!

"Sergeant," he squeaked, "Captain Adams tells me I'm to be your new platoon leader. By noon today I'd like to know exactly how many men we've got for duty, an ammo count, shower and recreation schedule, so forth and so forth — get me?"

"Yessir!" I said, kicking myself mentally for not having joined the Air Force. "Anything else, sir?" I cracked.

"Yes. We may as well inspect your positions now."

"Thank you, sir!" I said, aiming a second mental kick at myself.

"Don't thank me yet, Sergeant! Not just yet!" He

spun around and started up, slapping the stick against his leg.

If our new lieutenant liked anything about our sector, he didn't let me in on it. Still he wasn't exactly dry for words as we walked back down from the rifle pits toward the mortar positions. "That is" — he commenced — "beyond all doubt the worst mess I've ever inspected. And as for those smelly, unshaven, rumpled-up gold bricks you call a platoon . . ."

But that was only a beginning. That afternoon the center sector, which was our responsibility, was unusually quiet and, of course, "Georgie," as the boys had already started calling our cherubic new leader, didn't believe in just wasting time. By his orders I took every third man off the line and sent him down to shave and wash up. Then, while another third kept an eye on the Commies across the way, the final third began improving our positions.

I could have told our eager-beaver second-john that we were wasting time; that most of our action took place on night patrols; that during daylight hours nothing ever happened. We stood on a high, U-shaped stretch of land, some sixteen hundred yards opposite the Chinese, whose position was a straight, somewhat lower finger of white, grassy clay. We were sort of like an archery bow, with the Chinese finger stretched across our front, forming the string. The fact that our hills were higher than theirs gave us a natural advantage. **U. S. 1204409**

Yet it wasn't an easy sector. As soon as the sun started going down, one of the platoons would form up, eat a light supper, then wait for complete darkness. It was then the fun began. We knew the Commies were also forming up a platoon-size patrol to send out. Sometime between sundown and sunup these groups would be down in the bowl-shaped no man's land between the lines, playing a deadly brand of hide-and-seek. And not all those who went out would come back walking.

That was something our eager ex-hospital guard would soon have to learn. I figured he could learn it best by watching.

Later in the afternoon Georgie and I went up on the line for another look around. Every man jack was shaved raw by then, and scrubbed as clean as a helmetful of water and one rotating bar of soap could get them. "Well, Lieutenant?" I hinted, trying a grin for the heck of it.

"Well, what? Shall I put each of you in for the Medal of Honor because you look a little cleaner?"

With his swagger stick he kept hitting his boot as though he were a general or something. "Starting tomorrow," he told the men, "we'll start digging you up some clean fatigues. Also, I've sent for regimental patches from headquarters, and I'm personally donating two cans of polish for those crummy-looking brogans you're all wearing."

"Good gosh!" said Hoop Keeler. "We're gonna Mickey Mouse on the front lines?"

"Who's this man?" asked the lieutenant.

"Corporal Keeler," I said.

He didn't even face toward Hoop again. "Tell him to sew on some stripes, or at sundown he reverts to private. That goes for all your NCO's."

"Yessir!" I said. It was then that I got my first glimpse of the real George Poole. He could've added: "And that includes you, Sergeant." But he had not. And an old, unwritten Army rule came to my mind: "Never make a subordinate lose face before his men." There and then, on the unmistakable strength of that one small clue, the picture of a comical little shavetail playing parade-ground soldier before his men began to fade.

We were on the line again next morning when Lieutenant Poole first noticed our pride and joy. He was searching the lower area through field glasses, when suddenly he let out a yell.

"Jumping snakes! What's that?"

"What's what?" I asked him, enjoying the moment.

"Am I going crazy, or is that a house down there?"

Mel Roper, another of my corporals, laughed. "A house, sir?" he asked innocently while the other men turned away to suppress grins.

"And — holy snakes!" Poole turned to me. "Listen, Sergeant. I know I'm not nuts, but I just saw — There's an old Korean woman running around down there, hanging wash!" And he blinked. "Well, look — don't laugh!"

Corporal Roper was just kidding.

I told him: "Guess we just forgot to mention Mother Chin."

"Mother what?" he said incredulously.

"Mother Chin, sir. That's what the guys call her. She's just what you thought you saw. An old Korean lady."

His eyes grew wider. "An old Korean woman — a house — right dab smack in the middle of no man's land? What is going on here anyway, sergeant?" He turned, fixing the glasses on the tiny straw-and-mud hut below. "Oh, no!" he yelled. "A girl!"

"Yessir," I said. "That's Mother Chin's daughter, Little Chin-Chin."

"And who's coming out of there next — Mao Tse-tung?"

"No, sir," said Roper seriously. "That's all there is."

"Does Captain Adams know about this?" asked Poole.

"Yessir, he does. Fact, he sometimes comes up here to watch them hang wash. We all do. It's very nice," I said.

"Oh, it's very nice, is it? And some of you don't by any chance ever drop down for a spot of tea, or to help them wring out the sheets, do you?"

None of us answered, because he was so mad he looked ready to bust.

At last his cherubic red face came back to its normal freckled white again. "How long's this side show been going on?"

"About six months, sir," I told him. "The hut — or most of it — was down there when the Third Battalion pushed the Commies off this range to that lower one ahead. Some of their mortar and arty had hit it once or twice, but never bad. Then one morning, very early, the Third Battalion guys spotted this old Korean mamasan and her daughter — least they guessed it was her daughter — making for the old hut, balancing everything they owned on their heads. First thing you know, the Chinks drop a couple of mortar shells near them; maybe for fun. Anyway, the Third Batt didn't take to that kind of fun, so they gave the Commie lines back about twenty rounds. And that did it. Nobody has ever bothered the old dame and her kid again."

"Well, somebody's sure going to bother them now!" said the lieutenant. "C'mon, Sergeant. We're going to have a talk with Captain Adams — right now!"

If Georgie Poole thought Adams was going to be on his side, he was soon disillusioned. Not only did the skipper not take to Poole's side, but he definitely ordered him to leave the Chins alone.

"Leave 'em alone, Captain?" he screeched. "Why, how do we know who they are? The Chinks might've even put 'em there!"

"I appreciate your enthusiasm, Lieutenant," our company commander said. "But you're way off base this time, believe me." And he laughed. "Why, to touch them would be practically violating a tradition. Besides, they're harmless. We've observed them closely for months — ever since we inherited them from the Third Batt."

"And how do the Commies feel about them, Captain?" he asked.

The captain looked at me. "How about it, Sergeant?"

"Well, Lieutenant," I said, "they must feel pretty much the same. You know, sir" — I felt suddenly foolish, but I went on — "it's a funny thing. That old lady, and that poor kid with her — well —"

"Well, what?"

"Well, the guys on the line have sort of adopted them. It's not so unusual. I've known other cases of these poor people wandering back to homes which are still in the combat area. They're very simple. They just don't understand war."

"And I've known of their being blown to bits too!" said Poole.

"Oh, no," laughed Captain Adams. "Not on this front, Lieutenant! Not by the enemy either. Mother Chin and little Chin-Chin are a sacred institution to both sides."

Lieutenant Poole didn't say any more, but was dismissed. He saluted, and led me out of the captain's dugout muttering, "Of all the silly poppycock . . ."

"The captain was saying what we all feel, sir," I told him.

"The captain's my superior and I won't contradict him, because I'm a soldier," he said. "But tradition or not — civilians they are, and civilians don't belong in the combat zone."

That afternoon we took one of our periodic pastings from the Commie mortars, with the usual dirty results. We had three wounded. Among the five boys killed by a direct hit on a mortar position was Sergeant Shoskovitch, a buddy of mine. We lobbed about ninety rounds back at them and Captain Adams ordered our heavy machine guns to sweep every suspected position. But it didn't bring back our dead boys.

Watching from above, I saw Mother Chin run around, scared half to death, before she got sense enough to jump into a hole nearby. Poor little Chin-Chin was probably in the shack yet, cringing under something. But the oddest, saddest part of it was seeing that pitiful, ragged laundry hanging on a make-shift line between the hut and a shrapnel-shattered tree.

"Poor old woman!" I said aloud, despite myself. Then I turned and noticed the lieutenant's eyes on me.

Well, the heck with you, Georgie, I thought to myself.

That evening the first platoon sent out a patrol, it being their turn on the round-robin schedule. It was the same old story. In the morning, Lieutenant Donovan returned, nursing a scratched arm, and with three men wounded seriously, and two dead. I accompanied Poole to officers' briefing that afternoon.

"We went down by the camouflaged cut," Donovan reported. "Then proceeded undetected through our minefield —"

"Excuse me," interrupted Poole. "Is the Chink area mined too?"

"Yes," said Donovan. "But we know the layout, and we also shell a path through before we start down. Our mortars are pretty good at that." Then he went on. "We were fine going past Mother Chin's. The joint was blacked out, but we could hear them muttering inside. Then we proceeded another one hundred yards — and the Commies gave it to us: first it rained mortar shell, then we got machine guns."

"Boxed in again?" asked Adams.

"Yessir. Same-same. We couldn't go forward, we couldn't bug-out. The fire wasn't from their lines either. It came from a patrol, but well directed. When we began pulling out we got mortar fire — two hits right on the trail! I mean right on! Killed two of my boys!"

"I saw the kids," said Poole. "Looked just like mines."

Donovan shook his head. "Nope. Couldn't have been mines. We took the same way back. No mines there."

An hour later Poole and I were up on the line, and the brash little looey was studying the layout ahead, when suddenly he seemed to read my mind. "The men don't much like my attitude, do they?"

"No, sir." I told him. "They don't."

"Is it that house down there — or is it something else?"

"Lieutenant, I don't want to be disrespectful," I told him, "but if you're asking me —"

"I'm asking you — and I'm ordering you! Go ahead, lay it out."

"That house is all they have," I said. "You've been to see the captain again about it, haven't you?"

"That's right. I have. And I'll keep on seeing him!"

"Why?"

"Because it's a menace, that's why!"

"Because you're the kind of man who just can't

leave things as he found them!" I finally exploded. "That's why!"

"So it's going to be war between us, after all," he said.

For an instant his freckled little face seemed somehow sad.

"I'm your subordinate," I said. "I'm only an enlisted man, but contrary to popular opinion an EM can think and feel. And another thing, Lieutenant. You came out of a guard detachment three miles back of the lines. Came out to these poor devils and started in pushing your spit-and-polish ideas. Well, they're soldiers — front-line soldiers — and they're proud of it."

"And they can't be proud, now that they're clean?" he said evenly. "They can't be proud any more because they look like soldiers, and not like ragpickers — is that it?"

I didn't answer him, because I didn't know how.

"All right," he went on. "Ever since I got here, you and your little band of heroes have been chewing your nails to the knuckles, wondering who I am, what I am, and what I intend to do. So I'm going to put you out of your misery. I'm going to tell you." He sat against the sandbags, took his polished swagger stick in both hands, and sighed deeply. "You know my name, my rank, my serial number. You know me as a homely runt. You probably figure I'm a PX commando with a Napoleonic complex and a gripe against anybody taller than I am — which is nearly everybody —"

"Lieutenant," I said, "I guess I shouldn't have —"

"You listen," he said dryly. "I think this is the dirtiest, most fouled-up outfit I've ever seen. You people make me sick. You run around playing long-range peeping-Tom and getting all teary-eyed about a lot of unprofessional malarky: carrying on as though the whole universe hangs on what happens to that filthy little hut down there! Well, it doesn't."

"So you're a professional soldier," I said sarcastically, because I was sore.

"That's right! That's exactly right, Sergeant."

"Then why were you so busy playing soldier boy back there instead of coming up here to fight before this?" I snapped.

"Fight?" he said. "Fight, did you say?" He ripped open his fatigue jacket, showing me a bluish, just-healing bullet scar in his chest.

"I'm sorry," I said. "I didn't —"

"I know," he said, a little calmer. "Brand-new

second lieutenant. Where does he come from? Who cares? He's a stiff-back punk, straight out of a cush job. He carries a silly swagger stick. He makes us wash up and dress up and polish our boots. So he's a regular punk." He picked up the stick and cleaned it off on his leg. "Shall I tell you why the EMs hate — or at least suspect — an officer on sight? It's because he is pledged to make them go against every healthy, normal, decent instinct they possess. His job is to make them kill. To expose them to death or injury. To kick them in the pants when they'd rather have sympathy. To make them work when they'd rather just sit in the mud feeling sorry for themselves."

"Is it all right if I smoke?" I asked.

"Go ahead. No, thanks. I don't use them."

"They'd cut your wind?"

"Something like that," he admitted. "Why aren't you an officer? You're a college man, aren't you?"

"Yessir. University of Southern California."

"You're a good NCO," he said. "You know your job; you're quick. But you're a snob. You feel you're too good to wear bars, don't you?"

"Yessir," I said.

"Well, I don't. I'm not a college man. I'm a farmer's kid who hated farms and loved the Army. And I'm a

darned good soldier by anybody's standards, because
I know what I'm supposed to do — and I do it without sentimentality. I'm not too good to be an officer
— I'm just too good to be a second lieutenant.
Well, rank is frozen, so at least you must know
that I'm not doing all this to get a promotion, don't
you?"

I had to laugh. "Lieutenant," I said, "you'd make
some diplomat!"

"All right," he said, rubbing his face wearily. "It's
all been said, except one last thing: I think the Chinks
planted that sweet little family down there; and, one
way or another, they're going to go!"

I threw my cigarette down and stepped on it.
"We'll see."

"That's right, Sergeant. We'll see."

The house and its two occupants became almost an
obsession with Lieutenant Poole after that. On his first
patrol, he was making his usual thorough check of
equipment, when he spotted the sandbag I was
filling.

"What's that?" he asked.

"It's a little extra chow," I told him.
"What for?"

The men and I looked at him. "It's for Mother Chin and little Chin-Chin," I told him. "It's a tradition. When we go through the minefield, we always pass the hut, and the patrols throw over a few C-rations, maybe some jam."

"Put it back," he said sternly.

"Lieutenant —"

"That's an order, Sergeant."

After that his stock hit somewhere below zero. Even Roper and Keeler and the other squad and section leaders, who'd tried to go along with him, were cussing him out privately. Even the other officers, including Captain Adams, were hard-put to be civil to him.

"I see you didn't tell them about my suspicions," he said a few days after the patrol.

"No, sir," I said. "And I'm not going to, either."

"That's your privilege," he said.

I had to admit one thing, though. He'd done a first-class soldiering job out there in the dark, dangerous night. If anything, he'd surprised me by being as cagey and cautious as they came. I'd rather expected him to *gung ho* his way headfirst into danger. But when the Chinese sprang their ambush, Poole had already backed us out of it sufficiently to disengage without serious results. Then he'd insisted on leading the way back himself, poking the marked path through the minefield with a bayonet all the way.

But what was stranger yet was that next morning I'd been called up to the Old Man's dugout, and there I'd seen Lieutenant Poole, his face still red with anger and frustration, while the captain's didn't look much happier.

"Sergeant," the captain said. "Lieutenant Poole claims that last night he found two mines in the return path of the platoon. What do you know about that?"

I shook my head, surprised. "Nothing, sir. Nothing at all."

"Well, that does it, Poole!" he said angrily. "It seems you're the only one who saw any mines — and that's not enough for me. Now, I'm telling you for the last time: Lay off the Chins! *Lay off* — get me?"

"You mean let them go on butchering people — *our* people? My men?"

"If you're sorry enough to begrudge a helpless old woman and a skinny, underfed girl their miserable living and their only home — then that's what I mean," exploded Adams. "Exactly what I mean!"

"If you'll listen, sir, I'll tell you —" he began.

"Get out!" yelled Adams. "You're dismissed! Both of you!"

Little Poole was beet-red and breathing like a buffalo when he stomped out. I followed him, feeling a mixture of gladness and maybe a tinge of pity at how things had turned out. At least it was over.

At the top of our position Poole leaned his head against the edge of a sandbag emplacement, pounding a fist hard into the dirt. "That — that stupid, stupid —" But seeing me beside him he couldn't go on, I had to say that for him. He was a mean little tyrant in many ways, but even half crying with rage, he couldn't belittle the captain in front of me.

"Please, Lieutenant," I said soothingly. "It's no use!"

"Oh, isn't it?" he said between clenched teeth. He lifted his binoculars and put them on the house below. "Look at them!" he said. "They're at it again!"

I raised my own glasses and focused on the hut. It looked as peaceful and quiet as a scene on a calendar painting. To one side Mother Chin stood, her skinny, sad, half-stooped figure reaching for her pile of ragged laundry which she was hanging to dry. Just in front of the door, little Chin-Chin sat mixing something in a bowl, as if resting in the warm sun.

"The dirty butchers!" he said vehemently. And then he turned to me and said quietly, "I'll bet you we get a royal pasting by mortar fire within another hour. Will you bet?"

"Why —"

"Will you?" he growled in his comically high voice. "Will you bet that somebody dies? That we drag out torn, bleeding kids from holes bashed in by direct hits within one hour?" Even for Poole the power of his anger was almost terrifying. The hatred was so strong within him that his eyes had turned red-rimmed and he was breathing in gasps. He scared me! He really scared me!

But he was right. An hour later Keeler was dead. His big, loose-jointed body lay twisted beside that of two others. I would never hear him again. I would never see his homely face break into one of his slow grins. The thought of it choked me up, but it was nothing to what it did to the lieutenant.

"You — you couldn't have known this for sure," I said.

"I knew it sure as we're standing here," he told me. "I let them kill him — but they'll never kill anyone

else again. Not here — not on patrol. Not ever, anywhere again!"

At dinnertime I saw him sitting near the kitchen
fly, with the other officers, hardly looking at his chow.
He sat there looking so little, so kidlike; ostracized,
ignored. I'd never felt so sorry for anyone in my life.

It was Donovan's turn to take out a group that
night, and I was nearby when Lieutenant Poole
walked up and asked to take his place. Donovan just
looked down at him as though he had been dirt. "The
answer's no," he told him.

"But I've got to get down there."

"Listen," Donovan said. "Why don't you wise up,
mister? The men don't like you, the officers don't like
you — and I don't like you! Why don't you go find
yourself a hole somewhere?"

"I didn't come here to be popular," Poole said without flinching. You had to hand it to the little bantam:
big Donovan didn't scare him a bit. "And what you
personally care doesn't ring any bells with me, either.
I asked to take your patrol out tonight."

"And I said no!" Donovan told him.

"Then at least let me tell you ——"

Donovan threw him a dirty look, then turned his
back and walked off.

"You fool!" said Poole angrily. "You blind fool!"

It was the custom for the patrol leaders to take their men out before moonrise, which would be generally about 2100 hours — or nine o'clock. At a little past eight I realized that Poole was gone. For a moment I felt my belly shrivel up, and a near-panic gripped me. My God, he's gone to kill them! I thought, breaking into a run for Poole's bunker. Sure enough, his pistol, his helmet and a spare submachine gun were gone. I ran to the top of the line, hunting for Roper.

"Roper, Roper!" I called.

"Yeah? What is it?" said Roper, coming out of a machine-gun pillbox.

"Lieutenant Poole — have you seen him?" I saw that he was stalling, and I grabbed and shook him. "Answer me!"

In the darkness his barely discernible face looked surprised. "Yeah, Sarge," he said. "He come by here a while ago, lugging a chopper and a big load of grenades. Looked like he was going to a revolution or something. But —"

"But nothing!" I said. "Where did he go? Where, you meathead?"

"He'll bust me lower'n a snake's belly, but — He

went on down. He went down by the covered approach. Out toward the Chink lines."

I ran. I ran hard as I could and found Lieutenant Donovan, who was still putting on his gear. I busted into his bunker and panted: "He's gone, Lieutenant! Poole's gone to kill the Chins!"

"What're you saying?" he yelled. "Are you nuts?"

"No, sir! He's gone down alone, to get them. He's snapped his cork. He thinks the Chins have been killing our men somehow. We've gotta go after him, sir! He'll <u>kill them</u>! He'll do it, so help me!"

In the candlelight I saw Donovan turn white, then he threw on his things. "If this is a wild-goose — No. He's nutty enough to do it! C'mon! We'll round up the men and start right now!"

There wasn't time even to notify the skipper that we were going. We ran the patrol uphill, then cleared the lines and started down under the chickenwire and burlap which camouflaged the trench to no man's land. Then we went as no patrol has ever gone before.

But we were too late. Halfway across we heard the first explosion, then another and another, then a long burst from a Russian burp gun, followed by that of a tommy gun. Then there was a sheet of flame; a grenade explosion that seemed to blast the tiny hut apart in the pre-moon night. Then burst after crazy burst of machine-gun fire.

"He's done it!" cried Donovan, aghast. "The dirty, murdering maniac's done it!" With that a fury seemed to fill every last man of us, and we ran forward, crazy for our own revenge.

In a moment it all became a madhouse; a nightmar-ish, whirling free-for-all. The firing was all over the hut, and there wasn't just one gun, but guns were blazing from everywhere. And they weren't our guns. I threw myself into it, hardly thinking, and firing twice, I heard a Chinese grunt and fall. Then some-one swirled past me, and I heard Donovan yell: "Com-mie patrol! Commence firing!"

Running, I shot my way into the house as the big white moon broke from cover, and for a moment the light of it bathed the one room with a pale, almost blinding light. Behind the open door lay Mother Chin, dead.

Only she wasn't she any more. Her long Korean skirt was up and her head wrap was off. Mother Chin was shaved absolutely bald. She wore wrap-leggings and blue pants, and was still clutching a burp gun in one hand. Ten feet away lay little Chin-Chin, also quite dead, also bald under the bullet-torn head wrap. He had been perfect for the part: as beardless a teen-aged Chinese as ever you'll see. He, too, had gone down firing his submachine gun. Poole had certainly been thorough.

I ran out, looking for Donovan. A few trigger-happy kids were still pouring fire into the bushes, but the fight was over. A few feet off the trail I found him kneeling beside Poole, who lay bleeding, only half-conscious. "You wait till you're well!" Donovan was saying through his teeth. "You just wait — you lousy —"

"I think you'd better go look at Mother Chin and her little Commie offspring," I said, kneeling beside them.

"What did you say?" Donovan asked as though I were crazy.

"I said — hurray for Georgie Poole!"

In the half-light the little officer tried to raise his head, and for the first — and last time — I saw him smile. "Hurray for Georgie Poole," he repeated weakly. "Now let's get out of here!"

I saw Lieutenant Poole next morning as he was being carried down to meet the ambulance jeep. It would take him to a helicopter field just beyond mortar range, and then the hospital again. But I wasn't there alone. As many of the men and officers as could make it — including Captain Adams — were there to see him off, and as usual he didn't seem to give a hoot.

By then we all knew the story: he had given it to us, bit by bit, as the pain of two burp-gun slugs through a thigh and arm would permit. It had seemed so clear then. His reasoning had been simple, but direct: Why did just two women who never went anywhere have such a big wash so often? The answer we discovered by sending down a daylight patrol to collect the "wash." On the back of each piece had been painted a Chinese character which could be read through field glasses from the enemy side. Co-ordinates, ranges, changes in firing data for the mortars. The catch was that during daylight the Chinese needed somebody up close to spot movements. Someone who could move around freely "gathering wood," for example. Our mistake was that we had always thought of communication in terms of wire or radio, either of which we would have spotted in a hurry.

"Their mistake," Poole added, "was that they got overly ambitious and started setting mines in the trail to catch our returning patrols. They counted on our thinking it was mortar fire which was killing our men. But there was no shrapnel in the bodies I saw. It had to be the Chins. Don't you see?"

We saw it. Saw it clearly enough to put Lieutenant Poole in for a medal, with all of us signing the recommendation. And Captain Adams saw it enough to offer his hand in apology to the tough little guy, who took it silently, without a trace of softening.

Then they were gone back to their jobs up there, and only Poole and I remained behind. I looked at him as he lay, in pain, flat on a stretcher that was shoved atop the ambulance jeep. Then I took my cigarettes, lighted one and offered it to him.

"You won't need your wind where you're going," I smiled.

"Back to that dull meat factory again," he said, taking it. "You keep on these guys," he told me sternly. "Bear hard on them. Give 'em pride. Keep them alive!"

"Yessir," I replied. "I'll do that. And —"

"And what?"

"And you're one heck of a nice guy — sir," I said.

"You think so, eh?" he said, sourly as ever.

"I know so, Georgie," I told him.

He looked at me mutely for a moment, then nodded. I knew in how much agony he must have been, but he hadn't moaned once. "Just don't let it get around," he whispered. Then he raised his squeaky voice. "All right, driver! Let's get this buggy going. I could've walked to that hospital by now!"

As they drove away, his head turned and he looked at me. I waved, but his expression never changed. It was his way. And his way was good enough for me.

The Wrong Way
to Win a War

by John Godey

EXCEPT for the loss of Sergeant Piccone, the lieutenant reflected, the mission of the patrol, such as it
was, had been accomplished without serious mishap.
And he was no more than grudgingly thankful that
"loss" did not carry its usual tragic connotation. It
meant simply that the sergeant had been misplaced
and must be found before they could return to base.

Personally, Lieutenant Aylward didn't care if the
sergeant was never found. Nor, for that matter, did he
care if his searchers, who were starting to fan out into
the woods, beating the brush noisily like so many Boy
Scouts hunting for a strayed child, all managed to get
lost too. Indeed, it could only benefit mankind in
general, the Army specifically, and Lieutenant Aylward in bright particular, if the entire patrol, together
with Sergeant Piccone, should fall into some con-

venient hole and vanish forever. He shrugged his carbine from his shoulder, cradled it in the crook of his arm, and watched in silent rage as his little squad clumped heavily into the dappled foliage. It occurred to him, with that feeling of helpless exasperation which the past weeks had hardened into a permanent mood, that his men would doubtless balance the finding of the sergeant by losing some major item of government issue; probably, if they ran true to form, the most expensive and critical.

He regretted not having ordered Ostermuller to leave the BAR behind when he went off.

They were out of sight now in the brush, but not out of earshot. The woods resounded with the clamor of laughter and curses and an occasional loud shout.

"Piccone! Hey, Mario, where you at?"

"Sarge! Hey, Sarge!"

"Come out, jerk, come out, come out, wherever you are. . . ."

Aylward winced, as much for the unsoldierly nature of the sounds as for the utter disregard of the ordinary discipline of silence, and thought: If there is a Red formation anywhere within a ten-mile radius, they'll think they've trapped an entire company. The notion was suddenly startling, and it alerted him to a troubled awareness of his responsibilities. He brushed aside his irritation and gazed about him at the brutal Korean terrain, studying it with professional attention to detail.

To the left, wearyingly familiar, were the inevitable rice paddies. His mind automatically registered the fact that they were reasonably protected from a surprise attack in that quarter. Directly behind him was a culvert, now dry, which must once have served as a drainage ditch for the rice paddies. Beyond the culvert, continuing southward, were the miles of dusty, sparse farmland they had traversed earlier to reach this point. His mind veered away abruptly from the possibility that an enemy patrol might have managed to circle and slip behind them.

To his right, perhaps a hundred yards off, was a high, freakish bluff. Its face was perpendicular and unbroken except for a broad, rock-strewn cleft in the center, which ran up at a twenty-degree gradient for a distance of about two hundred feet before it ended raggedly against the sheer continuation of the wall. The cut obviously represented an attempt, which had been abandoned, to quarry the bluff. Aylward noted a breastwork of boulders two thirds of the way up, marked it automatically as a beautiful defensive posi-

tion, and turned again toward the wood. There was
no longer any sound to be heard within it.

He shifted his carbine and fretted and felt sorry for
himself. Although he was hardened in the ways of the
Army and knew that the shuffle of the cards was
sometimes of necessity bizarre, he resented being dealt
from the bottom of a marked deck. The fact that he
might have avoided the role did not lessen his indignation at finding himself the chaperon of the lousiest six
in the lousiest squad in the lousiest platoon in the
lousiest company . . .

If he experienced an inward twinge at this inversion
of the familiar litany of service *esprit de corps,* he
could vindicate himself with the reminder that it was
an invention of the men themselves, who exploited it
constantly. That they actually took pride in their own
ineptitude seemed to Aylward the most conclusively
revolting fact of all.

He had probed himself repeatedly, searchingly, to
determine whether he must accept some part of the
failure as his own. At twenty-four he was a year or
two older than his men. Like them, he was a reluc-
tantly transplated civilian: The ROTC training which
had started him on the way up to his commission was,
in his university, compulsory. But he believed in fac-

ing necessity squarely, and he had made of himself as capable a soldier as it was within his power to be.

The Army had tried to do as much for the men, but they had deliberately refused the gambit. They defied all attempts to do so, derided them, and took pleasure in their ignorance and incompetence. The lousiest six in the lousiest squad in the lousiest platoon . . . They had begun by bewildering him and ended by defeating him. He believed now that they were a different breed from anything he had ever known.

He stiffened as a bright, moving patch flashed behind the greenery. It grew larger and became a figure pushing aside the boughs of a scrubby tree and stepping out into the open. It was Sergeant Piccone.

The sergeant blinked in the bright, cold sunlight, then lifted his hand in a sign of recognition and started forward at a dogtrot, his raincoat, looped loosely through his cartridge belt, flapping against his rump at each step.

He was dark and wiry, with an air of fierce but meaningless intensity, and he had the wrinkled, starved face of a jockey. He looked at Aylward with sulky accusation. "What's the idea going and getting lost on me?" he said.

Aylward was not in the least surprised that Piccone

— who owed his rating not to any superiority over the others, but to an inflexible Table of Organization, which insisted that so many sergeancies *must* be distributed — had decided everybody had gotten lost but him. It was the way they were. Nothing was ever their fault. It was the fault of someone else, of secret enemies, of a discriminatory fate. He was silent, because he knew there was no use in trying to change the sergeant's mind.

"We must have been three miles deep in them woods," Sergeant Piccone said, aggrieved. "I had a terrible time finding my way out. I had to shoot an azimuth." He pronounced it "azmut."

Aylward said in surprise, without ironic intent, "You really did? And it got you here?"

"It sure didn't get me to Michigan Avenue," the sergeant said. "Where's the rest of the gang?"

"Where are the *men*," Aylward corrected him. And then he thought: I'm just being technical; the sergeant is right — gang. "I sent them into the woods to look for you," he said.

The sergeant groaned. "You want I should go back after them?"

"My God, no!" Aylward said.

"I know them guys. They'll get lost again. There

ain't one of them clowns knows how to shoot . . .
an azimuth."

Later Aylward was to remember, with something
like childish wonder, that the rifleshot rang out pre-
cisely at the instant that the sergeant pronounced the
word "shoot," and that he had paused momentarily,
less in surprise than in annoyance at the interruption,
before going on to finish his sentence. Now there was
another shot, two, three — and the sergeant turned
pale in belated comprehension.

Aylward pushed the safety of his carbine on "fire"
and started forward. Three men erupted from the
woods on a dead run. Lieutenant Aylward ran toward them. "Where's Ostermuller? Where's Gillis?"
he shouted.

They flung out their hands in the direction of the
woods, without slackening their pace, and dodged
around him. As Aylward ran on, there were more
shots. And then he saw Gillis burst out of the woods.
Behind him came Ostermuller laboring under the
heavy and awkward burden of the BAR. Aylward
saw them lower their heads in redoubled effort. Gillis
drew ahead, and went by Aylward in the direction
taken by Wilson, Marchese and Szymanowski. Ayl-

ward ran forward to meet Ostermuller, then reversed, and, running abreast of him with the tentative step of a relay runner awaiting the passing of the baton, swooped down for the muzzle of the BAR. Instinctively, using his hold on the BAR as a lever, he bore to the left, in the direction of the bluff. But the others were tumbling into the culvert straight ahead, and he veered back into line.

They were within five yards of the culvert when the first rifleshots rang out, and on its lip when a machine gun began its ferocious stutter. Aylward fell forward, dragging Ostermuller after him, and they sprawled joltingly on top of the others, the BAR wrenched from their grasp. Aylward rolled over on his knees and cautiously peeked at the woods, over the wall of the culvert.

The culvert erupted with the sound of voices. They were all talking at once, angry and frightened. "Reds . . . We come up on their bivouac . . . Must be a hundred . . . Lucky we saw them . . . Sentry fired and we ran."

Aylward stared at the dark line of the woods for what seemed a long time before he detected any movement. A bush swayed gently, imperceptibly, but its movement was against the wind. He nestled his cheek against the stock of the carbine. Suddenly the culvert exploded in a thunderous fury. It took Aylward a stunned five seconds to realize that the squad was letting go with everything they had, five M-1s and the BAR pouring out fire, empty cartridge cases flipping out into the trench.

"Cease fire!" he bellowed. "Cease fire!"

His rage stopped them. The storm of fire ended with the same abruptness with which it had begun. Glaring, Aylward turned, and at that instant Wilson stood upright. Aylward hurled himself forward, the helmet on his lowered head taking Wilson viciously at the knees and bringing him down. From the woods, the machine gun, too late, ripped off a short, ugly burst.

Lying sprawled across Wilson's legs, Aylward shouted, "You crazy idiot!"

Wilson pointed a shaking finger at him. "You assaulted me. I got witnesses. Striking an enlisted man. Wait'll the inspector general hears about this."

Aylward's indignation choked in him and became a wild strangulated laugh. He checked it abruptly and rolled over to the forward wall of the culvert. He studied the woods. The foliage was bright green in the sun, and the floor dappled, before it gave way to dark, motionless shadows. He turned away from it and looked at the men.

His voice was quiet, calm, but he could not quite filter out the overtone of grim satisfaction: "They're shooting live rounds at us, you know."

Gillis reeled off a string of meaningless epithets, then subsided. In the silence that followed, the sound of breathing was like that of a cageful of cornered animals. They stared at him numbly, their faces blank.

"We're going to do our best to make a fight of it," Aylward continued. "What you should have learned in basic training, and didn't, you're going to have to learn now under fire. And if you don't, I'll kill you myself. Any questions?"

There was a stirring of comprehension — nods, one or two "Yeah"s and even a frightened "Yes, sir."

After a moment he went on crisply. "First, we're going to try to set up some sort of effective firing line. Before long, we should be able to establish their number."

"At least two platoons, Lieutenant," Szymanowski said earnestly.

Ostermuller snorted. "I seen them. It's a whole company."

The discussion became general, and the ante was raised with each new estimate. Aylward silenced them with a curt command and gave brisk orders for the disposal of his little force. He set up the BAR in the center of the line, with Szymanowski, as assistant, to Ostermuller's left. Wilson and Gillis were also stationed at the left, Piccone and Marchese to the right of the BAR.

"Okay," Aylward said. "Keep under cover and *don't fire* until I give the command. When you get the order to fire, pick an individual target. And remember, hold your breath and squeeze the trigger, don't pull or jerk on it."

These were the elementary things, he thought, that they should have known at the end of their first month of basic training. It was doubtful that they had learned them or, in the short span left to them, ever would. It occurred to him, as he squinted up at the cool blue of the sky, that he would probably be dead before the day was over. It was not a prospect he could contemplate with equanimity. As a line officer of company grade, he was accustomed to admit to himself the eventuality — if not, normally, the inevitability — of dying in battle. But it seemed too bad a man couldn't choose the company in which to die; and it seemed a useless waste to die because a sergeant had got lost. But then, if the sergeant hadn't got lost, some other misfortune would have occurred.

Many months ago, when he had joined his new outfit, almost from his very first week as leader of the second platoon of Able Company, he had never doubted the association would end in disaster.

Lieutenant Aylward had seen combat within two months of the commitment of American field forces to action in Korea. He had fought hard on both sides of the 38th Parallel and in the drab, ruined streets of Seoul, and had been a mile or two from the Yalu River when he was wounded. A shell fragment had hit him in the back and lodged close to one of the lumbar vertebrae. He had been flown back to Tokyo. After the operation, which successfully removed the fragment, after his convalescence, after the vexing and anomalous period of rehabilitation — which combined the most tedious aspects of both hospitalization and active duty — he had been sifted into the replacement pipeline and assigned to his present outfit. It had already been alerted for Korea.

Other than a nagging premonition which he had set down to nerves, Aylward had had no real reason for misgivings. Outside of marching from one end of Camp Drake to the other at the head of the second platoon of Able Company on its dreary pre-embarkation rounds of medics, finance, orientation and supply — and observing that its members rated low from the standpoint of housekeeping and military courtesy — he wasn't able to take their measure in any important respect. But full knowledge was not long in coming, after they moved into their new base in a reserve area south of the then static front. It was the period of endless but still hopeful negotiation at Panmunjom. To keep the men occupied, the battalion S-3 had organized a month-long program reviewing the basic infantry training. For Aylward, this had been a staggering experience.

After a week, and at the end of a hideous day in which the platoon had committed every conceivable error — and a few that were quite inconceivable — in the execution of a simple problem in extended-order drill, Aylward threw in the sponge. The moment the platoon fell out, he hunted up the company commander.

"You're out of a National Guard outfit, Lieutenant?" the Old Man asked.

"Sir," Aylward said forcefully, "it's like living a

nightmare. They can't drill, they can't march and they can't shoot. They don't try, don't care —"

"— And they don't even speak a language you can understand?"

"What are they?" Aylward asked in genuine perplexity. "Imbeciles?"

"They're troops," the Old Man said somewhat sharply. "They're the citizens' army. And they're our responsibility, Lieutenant."

Aylward said, "Sir, I'd like to request a transfer."

The Old Man said slowly: "They're out of the big cities, the slums. They've been aware of enemies ever since they were old enough to walk. The cop on the beat, the schoolteacher — they regard anyone with authority as an antagonist. Now they've got a new enemy, the Army. They're fighting it in the best way they know: denying it, resisting it, refusing to become a part of it. They won't learn to shoot or drill or march simply because the enemy, authority, wants them to. We have to show them the Army isn't their enemy."

Aylward said doggedly, "Captain, I'm sorry, I'd like to request a transfer out."

"I won't endorse it, Lieutenant," the Old Man said. "I can't spare you."

Aylward shook his head hopelessly. "I can't fathom

what makes them tick, and I never will. They're approximately my own age, they're my own generation, but they come from another planet. There's no way I can get through to them."

The Old Man picked up a batch of morning reports from the field desk and shuffled them aimlessly. "All right. I'll tell you what I'll do for you. You've had a pretty bad wound, I understand. They're looking for an adjutant over at regiment. I'll endorse a request for —"

"No, thank you," Aylward said grimly. "I'm a field soldier."

The Old Man grinned. "Do your best, Lieutenant. You have my sympathy. Make soldiers out of them" — he looked up and met Aylward's eye — "or something," he concluded lamely.

Aylward saluted and went away. In a daze, he wandered back to the second platoon area. There was a crap game in progress, noisy with bickering, with the loud, intense, hard-bitten cries of the bettors. Beside the road, in a cluster, lay the Lousiest Six, their heads pillowed on their clumsy packs, their lips curled in permanent sneers as they gazed up at the unoffending sky in quintessential disgust.

One of them sat up, and Aylward recognized Private Marchese. He had the smooth olive skin, the round face and the narrow, clever eyes of a Renaissance intriguer. "Got a military-type argument for you to settle, Lieutenant," he said.

Aylward stopped. He said warily, "What's the problem?"

"It's a little discussion between me and the Brain." The nickname was their sardonic tribute to the ponderous, slow-thinking Ostermuller. "You know in military hygiene where it tells what steps should be taken when you close up a bivouac?"

"Yes?"

"Ostermuller don't believe me."

Aylward looked at Marchese's earnest face and he bit. "Well, what steps do you —"

"Why, thirty-inch steps, Lieutenant," Marchese said innocently.

The men on the ground burst into laughter, harsh and derisive, a laughter — Aylward thought, bitterly — that was meant to sting, to wound its object. Marchese did not abandon his solemnity. He continued to regard Aylward blandly, but his eyes were mocking.

Standing at the end of the mess line in the fading

twilight, Aylward questioned himself at length. Where had he failed? Why had he been unable to win their trust and affection? How had he earned their abiding scorn? He had tried to be a good officer, to impart to them his knowledge and experience, to share their hardships, to be just, to be friendly, to be kindly or paternally severe as the occasion demanded. But he had been unable to penetrate their tough, city-bred defenses. They regarded him as their enemy, as their prey. Their private name for him was "Cornball." For all his pains, he was a cornball, a square, a yokel from some tiny burg out in California.

Marchese, going by him, carrying his laden mess kit, said softly, "Thirty-inch steps," and behind him, the others — Wilson, Gillis, Szymanowski, Piccone, Ostermuller — laughed raucously, woundingly.

In the culvert, Aylward, peering steadily at the green curtain of the woods, thought he detected a flutter in the branches of a stunted tree. The flutter spread, like a ripple on water, and beside him a constricted voice rose in a frantic scream: "Here they *come!*"

The brownish uniforms sprouted like strange blossoms in the green of the foliage, then broke clear, al-

ready on the run. Aylward reckoned their number at
thirty. They came in two wings, leaving the center
vacant for their machine-gun and rifle fire. They ran
bent at the waist, heads lowered, yelling shrilly, their
bayonets fixed.

Aylward, tracking a running figure with his carbine, shouted hoarsely, *"Fire!"* and the sound was
wrenched from his throat and drowned in the roar of
gunfire. He heard the steady ripping sound of the
BAR, and he thought: The fool should be firing in
short bursts; he'll use up all the ammo, or cause a stoppage. He concentrated on his own shooting, working
the carbine coolly, seeing each successive target loom
up larger in the sights.

They had covered slightly more than half the distance to the culvert when they wavered, suddenly reversed their field, and raced back toward the woods
in a frantic retreat. A wild, triumphant shout rose
from the culvert. Aylward calmly sighted on a fleeing
Red, and the man fell forward at the edge of the
woods. Then they were all gone, and there was nothing to be seen but the still-quivering foliage.

"Cease fire!"

The patrol was shooting with unabated fury at
nothing. He shouted again and again, and at last was

forced to crawl the length of the culvert on his hands and knees, screaming at each one individually, tugging at their clothing, before they would stop. They slumped back from the wall and stared at one another in a daze. The machine gun in the woods fired a series of frenzied bursts, as though in frustrated rage, and then ceased.

Aylward counted six bodies lying in the dust. The attack had begun and ended in less than a minute.

In the culvert, the squad was celebrating a victory bigger than Waterloo, bigger than Agincourt or Gettysburg. When they had finished shouting and laughing and pummeling one another, they began to sound off individually.

Wilson said, "So this is combat. It's easier than shooting on the transition range. And you don't even have to polish up your brass."

Gillis scoffed at him. "Listen to old Maggie's drawers. We got them all, between me and the lieutenant."

Ostermuller said, "You guys give me a pain. Me and Shimmy knocked them off with the Browning."

"Right," Szymanowski said. "We mowed them down." He was a heavy-set Pole, with a thatch of thick blond hair that was his especial pride.

Marchese sneered. "Nobody hit nothing. They all died from the measles."

"Hey, Lieutenant," Gillis said, "lend me your knife so's I can notch my gun. I mean" — his sharp Celtic features became mock-penitent — "I mean my rifle, or piece. Never call it a gun."

Ostermuller said in his slow, rumbling voice, "I don't get a Silver Star out of this, I quit."

"Sure, you quit," Wilson said. "With a Section Eight you quit."

"Section Four," Marchese said. "Section Eight is for wholewits."

Sergeant Piccone screwed his gnomish face around to Aylward. "Why'n't you tell us it was this easy, Loot? Up to now you had us real worried."

Aylward did not bother to disillusion them. But he knew how lucky they had been. If the Reds had not turned back, they could not have failed to overrun the culvert. He thought it possible that they might have lost heart because the leader of the charge might have fallen. Or, more likely, they had not counted on facing a BAR, and the unexpected firepower had panicked them. In either case, they would not again risk a frontal attack.

What came next would not be so easy. He had a fair notion of what it would be.

It was nearly an hour since the enemy attack had been repulsed, and Aylward's nerves were jumping. To be sure, time — up to a certain point — was in their favor. But they had to stay alive to profit by it, hoping that the Old Man might eventually send out a searching party for them. Damn the Old Man anyway, he thought, recalling his own misgivings about the patrol and the Old Man's assurance that, in such a quiet sector, their chances of encountering any Reds were negligible. It had been the Old Man's notion that a recon mission in a "safe" area might have a bracing effect on half a dozen or so of the poorest soldiers in the platoon. As a theory, it had sounded fine. Too bad the Reds hadn't co-operated. And Aylward regretted the simple honesty which had led him to choose the Lousiest Six. The presence of even one competent rifleman would have been a comfort.

He couldn't understand what was taking the enemy so long. It was too much to hope that they would overlook so obvious a move. They had only to send half their force to their right, under cover of the woods, emerge in the rice paddies, and then advance cautiously into range and enfilade the culvert. The force in the woods would keep the men in the culvert pinned in place, and they would be sitting ducks for the enfilading fire.

Wilson addressed him: "Hey, Lieutenant, we going to stay in this smelly hole all day?"

"You have a suggestion for getting out of it?" he asked mildly.

"Me? I'm just a cog in the machine. You're the big leader. You make the suggestions."

They let loose their coarse, wounding laughter.

Szymanowski said, "Better hurry, Lieutenant, or we'll be late for mail call."

Marchese laughed. "You're a dumbbell, Shimmy. Today's the day you get a Dear John letter from your girl."

Szymanowski took offense. Marchese, his slanted eyes half closed in contempt, goaded him. The argument rose in pitch, and Aylward turned in exasperation to silence them. But his glance went by them, above them, and he saw a group of Reds running out into the farthest of the rice paddies. There were between fifteen and twenty of them. The mud of the paddy slowed them down, but their advance was steady, and they did not take cover because they were out of effective rifle range. There was a yell from behind. He turned to see Gillis put his rifle to his shoulder and squeeze off three shots. The line of Reds disappeared.

Gillis was ecstatic. "I knocked down the whole blanking line of them!"

"They're too far away," Aylward said wearily. "Hold your fire."

The Reds rose up in the paddy and came on again, treading on the green rice shoots, lifting their feet heavily out of the suction of water and mud.

Marchese, breathing hard, said, "They can shoot right down the alley."

There was no sound now in the culvert as the squad crowded forward, fascinated by the slow, deliberate advance across the paddies. As they watched, one of the brown figures gave a signal, and the Reds dropped suddenly out of sight. They were approaching effective range now.

Aylward threw a brooding look at the high bluff to his right and made his decision. They would have to try to make a run for it. They would be sitting ducks for the machine gun and rifles concealed behind the foliage, but anything was better than remaining where they were, trapped in a ditch.

Piccone let out a sudden exclamation. "I got an idea, Lieutenant!"

"Yes?" Aylward said absently.

"We can't get away because them guys in the woods got us pinned down. So why don't I toss a grenade —"

"Too far." Aylward shook his head. "If we had a grenade launcher . . . But you can't *throw* a grenade that far."

"Maybe *you* can't," Piccone said pointedly. "Because you toss them according to the book." He aped the shot-put-like lob that was standard procedure for throwing a grenade. "Who could throw anything like that? But if I haul off —"

"Don't throw it like a baseball," Aylward said, mechanically echoing the phrase used in training. He shook his head again. "You can't throw a grenade that distance. Even if you could, it would go off in midair."

"You never been in a rock fight," Piccone said earnestly. "When I was a kid, I was always in rock fights, and I got a great reputation for an arm. Maybe it goes off in the air if you throw it on a fly —"

"Parabola," Aylward corrected.

"But you let go a clothesline peg —"

Aylward started to say no, but didn't. Instead,

he said, "Okay, Sergeant, let's give it a try. All of you, pay attention."

They were to wait for the grenade to go off, whether in the woods or in the air (he did not trouble to reassert the certainty that it would be in the air), and at the instant of burst they were to leave the culvert and make for the cleft in the bluff, not stopping until they reached the breastwork of boulders. He pointed it out to them, tracing with his finger its oblique slant, which brought it in a line roughly parallel to the culvert. They were then, he went on — those of them, if any, who were still alive, he added parenthetically to himself — to hit the ground and stay there. Szymanowski and Ostermuller would carry the BAR. Gillis would carry the BAR bipod. Wilson would carry Szymanowski's rifle.

Piccone unhooked a grenade and pulled the pin, keeping his fingers tightly curled around the lever. He squirmed his shoulders like a pitcher loosening up, spat on the grenade, and rubbed it up between his hands. Then he shot upright in the culvert, his arm already cocked back, and let loose. From the woods, the machine gun began again. Aylward dragged Piccone down from the forward wall of the culvert, where the momentum of his throw had sent him sprawling.

They did not watch the flight of the grenade, and the burst seemed an incredibly long time in coming. They were out of the ditch before the detonation had ceased, scrambling on hands and knees over the lip of the culvert. Then they were all running, wildly, stumblingly, and Aylward wondered why they were not already dead, why the men in the woods were not firing.

It was not until his feet hit hard on the beginning of the upward slope that he heard the first shots. Beside him, in front of him, the straining efforts of the others seemed agonizingly slow and labored, a losing battle against the pull of gravity. He pounded on doggedly, veered sharply to skirt around a curious outcropping of rock that formed a shallow cave, and then he was flinging himself at the barrier of rock. He wriggled over it and fell flat, his chest heaving, sucking the air in great gulps. All around him were sounds similar to those he himself was making, the wheezing and squealing of lungs starved for air. He became aware that the machine gun had suddenly started to fire. Bullets were spattering against the protective boulders.

He rolled to his knees and crawled from one to the other of the recumbent, writhing figures. All were present. All were unhurt. He dragged himself to an embrasure in the barrier and peered down. From a flash of movement in the culvert, he realized that it had been taken over by the Reds who had come across the rice paddies. Then he looked at the woods, and he understood why the enemy concealed there had been silent until now. A great ragged gap had been torn in the foliage. The grenade, incredibly, had reached its target.

Behind him, Sergeant Piccone's voice, gasping, said: "It ain't for nothing I'm the sergeant in this crummy outfit."

They began to sound off as soon as they had recovered their breath.

"You don't comprehend, Mario," Marchese said. "You got a thick head on you. In training, you would get chewed out for throwing that grenade like a baseball."

"I didn't. I threw it like a rock."

"Like a rock is wrong too. Right, Lieutenant Aylward?"

Aylward flushed, meeting the bland mockery of Marchese's dark eyes. He said stiffly, "I've never felt happier at being proved wrong."

"See?" Marchese said. "You made the lieutenant happy, Mario."

Wilson said admiringly, "How's the old soupbone feel, Mario?"

"Could use a little linnamin' for a rubdown. Any you guys got a little linnamin' on you?"

"I got some neat's-foot oil," Gillis said. "It works great on rifle slings and rubber arms."

"Wise guy," Piccone said. "It don't pay to be no hero in this smelly outfit."

Szymanowski said, "Don't throw it like a baseball," and emitted a loud guffaw. The others joined in, as though at a signal, and the wild laughter reverberated against the bluff.

There was to be no quarter given, Aylward thought, and perhaps he deserved none. He had cited Scripture, and Piccone had proved that Scripture was wrong. But did this one success wipe out all the previous failures? Wasn't their predicament itself due to a flouting of that same Scripture? He shook his head angrily, as if to dislodge the futile inner argument that engaged him, and, peeking through the barrier, took stock of their new position.

It was evident enough that they were well protected from any but a direct frontal assault. With trained, seasoned troops — he thought wistfully of his old outfit — the position could be defended indefinitely. The many boulders scattered about on the slope of the cleft, potential cover for an attacking force, had to be listed as a debit. But this worried him less than the shallow cave twenty feet below them, which he had noticed on his upward dash. It was formed, simply enough, by an overhanging shelf of flat rock, like a roof. It was spacious enough for three or four men, and they would be protected from fire above.

A patch of brown moved along the culvert, but he did not fire. It was too difficult a target to warrant expending even a single round of their dwindling ammunition. He glanced at his watch. Now time had changed sides; it was their deadly enemy. There was perhaps an hour and a half left before darkness. Under cover of night, there was no way of holding the Reds off. Piccone squeezed in beside him. "What you looking at, Loot?"

Aylward indicated the shelf and pointed out its invulnerability to fire from the angle of their position.

"Stop worrying," Piccone said confidently. "Any Reds get up in there, I bomb them with a grenade. We're saved. Piccone does it again."

Aylward did not bother to disillusion him. He knew that the horizontal slope of the shelf extended

far enough outward to afford ample protection from
a grenade burst.

Ostermuller, his brow furrowed in concentration,
said, "I got a better idea. We plant the BAR a little
below the cave, behind a rock. Then it don't do them
no good to get in there, because the BAR got it covered."

Gillis snorted. "How do you get the BAR down
there alive?"

"He asks time out," Wilson said. "No shooting until the BAR is in position."

"This is war," Ostermuller said with dignity. "You
want to live forever?"

"The Brain is right," Marchese said solemnly. "He's
a military genius." He put out his hand. "Good luck,
Brain. I'll put a flower on your grave in Arlington
Cemetery."

Ostermuller pondered for a moment, then flung
Marchese's hand away from him. "Listen, I ain't the
only guy who can fire the BAR. I didn't mean —" He
stared in appeal at the circle of somber pitying faces,
then turned to Aylward. "What do I know about
military tactics? There's a thousand things wrong
with the idea. Right, Lieutenant? Tell them it stinks."

Aylward shook his head. "It won't work," he said. Ostermuller let out a great, sighing breath of relief.

Marchese grinned. "Okay, Brain. You just passed up a chance to be a national hero."

When the Reds came, Aylward grudgingly granted them credit for a good measure of intelligent preparation. They had apparently studied the terrain minutely, perhaps even assigned specific points of cover to specific men.

Six or seven of them jumped out of the culvert and raced at top speed across the flat. Meanwhile, every rifle in the culvert, as well as the machine gunner and other survivors of the grenade burst in the woods, directed a withering fire at the breastwork of boulders. The squad fired excitedly and erratically, Aylward included, and the attackers made the base of the slope without a casualty, losing themselves behind the rocks that strewed the cleft.

Aylward ordered cease fire. They had missed their opportunity to stop the sortie in its tracks. The next phase would be critical. He had not failed to note that the attacking Reds carried grenades at their belts, and he had little doubt that their objective was to gain the shelter of the rock overhang.

He felt a tap on his shoulder. "I can get one of them down there, Loot." It was Wilson.

Aylward shook his head. "A waste of ammo. They're too well covered."

Wilson pointed out a formation of rocks in the shape of a rough parallelogram. "I can get the guy in there."

"A bullet travels in a straight line. You can't hit him if you can't see him."

Wilson tilted his head to one side. "You ever play pool, Loot?"

Aylward was inclined to wonder if Wilson had ever done anything else, but he simply repeated, "If you can't see him, you can't hit him."

"Like I say," Wilson said serenely, "if you ever played pool, you know how to play a bank shot. Instead of you shoot the ball straight into the hole, you bank it off the cushion."

"I get it," Piccone said. "Ricochet. He's going to ricochet a bullet in a bank shot off the rock."

They were challenging Scripture again. But hadn't they earned that right? Aylward nodded, as much in affirmative reply to his own question as to Wilson, and said, "Okay. Three tries."

"You got a bet," Wilson said gaily. "Eight ball in the side pocket."

Wilson sighted, and the squad clustered around him, shouting encouragement. He fired, and Aylward heard the shell ricochet. He thought he detected a flash of brown behind the rock.

Wilson was shaking his head. "Figured the angle a little wrong." He fired again and was still for a moment, watching his target. "A shade too much English on that one."

"Your last shot," Aylward said.

Marchese said coldly, "Don't disturb the shooter, please."

Wilson sighted carefully and squeezed the trigger. There was a sudden scream, and after a moment an arm appeared, palm up, as if flung out in some final spasm from the shelter of the rock.

Wilson rolled over on his back. "Eight ball in the side pocket," he said, grinning. "Made the shot."

Aylward did not expect the Reds' maneuver. It took him by surprise. As the six men on the slope abandoned concealment and started their dash upward, another wave leaped out of the culvert and ran forward. The maneuver was nicely designed to divert and scatter the concentration of the defenders, and by the time he had fathomed its intention, he knew with dismay that it would succeed. He sensed the squad's confusion. He screamed an order to concentrate on the first wave, pumping his own carbine furiously, but he knew it was too late. He saw three of the brown-clad figures hurl themselves forward into the shelter of the overhang.

At the moment that he gave the command to cease fire, he heard, close beside him, the thump of a bullet into flesh, followed by a gasp and the heavy sound of a falling body. He turned away from the barrier.

Their luck, which had been very good thus far, had evened out now, Aylward thought. Gillis was lying doubled up, his knees drawn in to his stomach, his fingers clawing at his side. Ostermuller was sitting down, his big hands clasped over one knee. Beyond him, Wilson was slowly folding a handkerchief to his bleeding face. The others seemed to be unhurt. The Reds had made amends, Aylward thought, not only for their previous stupidity, but for their bad shooting as well.

He knelt beside Gillis, tearing at his first-aid pack. He pried gently at Gillis's fingers, not looking at the sharp, pale face twisted with pain, and pulled up his fatigue shirt. He found the wound, an ugly hole between the ribs. As he was fixing the compress in place, Gillis gave a long, weary sigh, and his eyes rolled upward into his head. Aylward picked up his wrist and felt the pulse. Satisfied, he quickly completed his bandage and covered it with Gillis's shirt. He crept over to Ostermuller, who sat with his head down, his eyes leaden with pain as Szymanowski worked on his wound. His kneecap had been smashed. Wilson had been creased just below the ear, and there had been a good deal of blood, but he was not badly hurt.

Marchese, working over Wilson, said in a finicky voice, "If there's anything I can't stand, it's the sight of an enlisted man's blood. Officers' stuff is nice and blue, and it don't smell. Right, Lieutenant? Your blood stinks, Wilson!"

In his mind's eye, Aylward could visualize the three Red soldiers in the shallow cave beneath the ledge. He saw them flattened against the wall, unhooking the grenades from their cartridge belts, peering toward the culvert, where their commander, like an artillery observer, would signal "overs" and "unders" and nurse them in on their target. He knew exactly the motion they would make when they were ready, extending an arm out at full length, crooking it sharply at the elbow as they lobbed the grenade back and up on a high looping arc — unless he could stop them.

And so his decision was taken calmly, and without hesitation, because that was the only way such a decision could be taken. There was no reasonable hope of success. He did not expect success. It was simply something that had to be done, because in his life he had somehow absorbed the lesson that dying was less important than *how* you died.

He heard Gillis moan. He crept quickly to him, raised his head, and tilted his canteen to his lips. Gillis drank thirstily, then clutched at his sleeve. "Tell me the truth, Loot," Gillis said hoarsely. "Am I dying?"

Aylward shook his head firmly. "It's a nasty one, but you'll be okay."

"Will I be evacuated back to Japan?"

Szymanowski snorted. "A flesh wound. They'll vulcanize it and have you back in the line in a week."

Piccone said, "Where's the justice? He'll get three months in Japan out of it. Because he's too stupid to duck a bullet."

Ostermuller groaned loudly. "He ain't the only guy wounded. My knee is shot off. I'll never dance again."

Marchese said, "Wilson here is the luckiest of all.

So they shot his ear off. So what? Every time he loses a piece of that face, his looks get improved."

Aylward said casually, "I'm going to want a big demonstration of firepower in a couple of minutes. I want it really poured on. Ostermuller, do you think you can work the BAR?"

"I can't rest no weight on the knee. I may wobble a little bit, but I guess I can handle it."

"Wilson?" Aylward said. "You okay?"

Wilson nodded, then grumbled, "You don't even get no relief in this Army when you're wounded."

"Gillis. You stay put. Keep out of the way —"

"The only good shot in the crowd?" Gillis said. Wincing, white-faced, he dragged himself to the barrier. "No hands I can shoot a gun better than these blankers."

"Rifle," Aylward said automatically.

"Rifle," Marchese said, mimicking his tone. "Don't you know, you poor shot-up blanker, the darn thing don't shoot straight if you call it a gun?"

Aylward ignored Marchese. He checked the magazine of his carbine, then exchanged it for Gillis's rifle. He withdrew Gillis's bayonet from its scabbard, slid the ring over the muzzle of the rifle and made sure the stud was firmly engaged. The men watched him curiously.

"What you got in mind, Lieutenant?" Piccone asked.

Szymanowski said in a confidential whisper, "He's going to get a half a dozen Reds on the sticker and make *shashlik*."

Marchese, his narrow eyes glittering, said, "You got something heroic planned, Lieutenant?"

Aylward did not reply. He was crouched tensely against the barrier, trying not to think, to empty out his mind. He was still calm, still not afraid, but he knew he could only remain that way by not allowing his mind to work.

Marchese said, "Forgive me, Your Excellency. Don't waste your valuable breath answering the foolish questions of enlisted men."

What was preventing him from telling them, Aylward wondered? Was it because they would consider it a cornball gesture, scoff at him?

"Okay," he said, and shrugged. "The Reds down under that ledge intend to start lobbing grenades up here. I'm going down and see if I can stop them."

A ponderous silence followed. Finally Piccone said,

"It's crazy. You'll get killed for sure. But if you're going — I mean, while we're talking —"

Aylward explained tiredly: He had to take the calculated risk that the first grenade would be inaccurate. This was less daring or quixotic than it might seem. The Reds in the cave would have to work blind and take guidance from an observer in the culvert. There would of necessity be an interval between grenades while they received corrections. He would take advantage of this interval to make his move, in order to lessen the chance that a grenade burst would catch him exposed on the slope.

Ostermuller said judiciously, "That makes sense."

Marchese laughed. "The Brain is with it. That proves it stinks."

"You have a better plan?" Aylward's lips were white, bloodless. "If not, keep your mouth shut!"

Marchese looked at him in surprise, then sneered. "It's your funeral."

Aylward's temper snapped. He broke toward Marchese, scrambling, his fists clenched, and Marchese squared away to meet him. They came together, clutching clumsily for each other, and then a grenade exploded below them.

Aylward pushed himself free of Marchese and

THE WRONG WAY TO WIN A WAR *99*

crawled frantically back to his rifle. He braced himself
tensely, with one hand on top of the barrier, and
screamed: *"Now! Everything you've got!"*

He vaulted the barrier, and then he was rolling, sliding, skidding down the rocky slope. He lost his balance momentarily, thrashed about wildly to regain
control of his fall, and was hit just as he righted himself. He felt the burning impact of the slug in his
shoulder, and then he had reached the hard, flat surface
of the shelf that formed the roof of the cave. He
hugged it for a moment, wincing at the sound of
bullets passing overhead, and then he rolled over the
edge, holding the rifle far out from his body to avoid
spitting himself on his own bayonet.

He landed heavily, jarringly, catching a fleeting
glimpse of dark, astonished faces, and he knew that
he had surprised them. He pushed upward to his knees,
and thrust the bayonet in a short jab at the groin of the
Red nearest to him. There was a piercing cry, and the
man fell away. He saw the other two turn toward him,
bewilderment still lingering on their faces, as though
they did not yet quite connect him with the frantic
signals of warning that must have been flashing from
the culvert.

He flailed crazily with his bayonet at the man nearest him, and missed. But the Red soldier, backing away, lost his balance. The third man broke for his rifle, stacked with the rifles of the other two against the inner wall of the cave. Aylward shot him in the back at point-blank range and saw him convulse and then drop like a stone. He whirled to face the remaining man, but he was too late. His rifle was knocked aside, and the man was on him, bearing him back with his weight. He fell twistingly on his back, the rifle flying out of his hands. The pain in his shoulder was like a hot, sudden flame, and he was conscious of having screamed at the moment of impact.

The Red soldier fell on him heavily, his face very close, a dark blur, his breath hot and stinking. He was small, but muscular and terrifyingly strong, and Aylward fought back against him as if against some unreal creature in a nightmare, threshing and heaving in panic fear. He thrust upward with the heel of his palm and felt it thud against his opponent's face, but he knew the blow was without force. His arm was brushed aside, and something clasped his throat, pressing his head back, bruising the swelling muscles, flattening the windpipe. He arched his body, making horrible noises in his effort to breathe, tearing at the rigid, constricting fingers at his throat.

Then there was a flat, broad knife poised above him, and he struck upward at it in desperation. His hand hit the Red's wrist, deflected it for an instant, and then the blade recoiled and began its downward arc. There was a heavy jolt across his body, and the Red fell smotheringly across his face. The pressure on his throat was released.

He pushed against the intolerable weight of the Red, but it was mere weight, not force, and it yielded. Then he was free of it, and in its place, floating above him like a reflection blurred by water, was Marchese's face. Then he was being lifted, and Marchese was propping him up, steadying him.

Marchese shouted into his ear: "Let's get out of here!"

The Red fire, which had been held up during the brief struggle, now resumed. With Marchese pushing him, Aylward skirted the rim of the cave and started up the slope. He scrambled upward on all fours, not conscious of his pain now, sweat scalding his eyes, driven by the strength of his fear. He became aware, dimly, that the fire from behind the barrier had thinned out; the BAR was silent. The thought flashed and was gone, and he scrambled upward, sobbing, making desperate, inarticulate noises in his bruised throat. The barrier loomed up, and as he fell across it, as hands dragged him over it, he knew that he was hit again. He lay on his face, feeling the running of blood down his thigh.

He rolled over on his back, and his eyes searched the numb faces that looked down at him. "Marchese!" he said, and his voice was hoarse. "Where is —"

Sergeant Piccone was crying. Tears coursed down the furrows and hollows of his pinched face, etching new, shallow paths in the dirt that covered it like a yellow mask.

Aylward dragged himself to the barrier, the left side of him — the wounded shoulder and thigh — wooden and useless. He pulled himself up and peered through an embrasure. Marchese lay a dozen feet below, face down, his body loose and sprawling, like an abandoned sack. He dropped back and covered his face with his hands. Piccone was kneeling beside him, with a first-aid pack in his hand. Then he remembered the silent BAR. He wrenched himself around savagely and glared at Ostermuller.

"Tell me," he said through his clenched teeth. "Did you run out of ammo?"

Ostermuller shook his head. "The trigger thing —"

"I thought so!" Aylward said in a rage. "A stoppage. A simple stoppage, and because you never bothered to learn when you were training —"

He stopped. Ostermuller, looking more puzzled than usual, was cradling the rifle in his lap, and the fingers of his right hand were bloody. There was a smear of blood on the battered trigger-housing assembly.

Aylward apologized with his eyes. "I'll bring Marchese in," he said wearily.

Using his right hand, he started to haul himself up the barrier. Piccone pleaded with him. Aylward ignored him and concentrated on the barrier. Then Szymanowski lunged at him and knocked him flat. He flailed at Szymanowski and managed to get his right hand on the barrier again, and then a preposterous thing happened. Marchese came leaping over the barrier in a wild, tumbling fling of arms and legs.

Aylward began to laugh. He was still laughing, somewhat hysterically, when he started to drag himself toward Marchese. And he thought: It's all a conspiracy; they're not real; they're made up out of somebody's head. There was no other way to explain how they could come back from the dead.

He heard Marchese's gleeful voice: "I used the old head. I fell and slid halfway down toward the cave. I knew that I couldn't make it. So I stayed where I was and played dead, figuring they wouldn't waste bullets on a stiff."

Aylward bent his face down and stared at Marchese.

Marchese grinned slyly. "They teach you that in the manuals, Lieutenant?"

The sky was dark and lowering, with clouds like diluted ink everywhere but in the west, where light glowed brilliantly and eerily. Through the murkiness, Aylward could mark the Reds' position in the culvert only by the occasional flash of a rifle, a pale-yellow flash in the gathering gloom. In less than a quarter of an hour, it would be dark and there would be no way to stop what they couldn't see.

He took stock of their weapons. The BAR was useless. He had abandoned Gillis' M-1 in the cave, and Marchese had lost his when he had fallen on the slope. That put their entire armament at three rifles and a carbine, with perhaps a dozen clips and magazines left in all. Piccone and Marchese alone were unhurt. Gillis was unconscious again; Ostermuller had been hit twice. Wilson and Szymanowski, who had suffered a grazing wound in the chest, would be able to function reasonably well. As for himself . . .

He said, "I don't know whether or not they're in the mood to accept a surrender, but —"

The tired voices came to life, mouthing obscenities that floated away angrily on the chill air. Under cover of the gloom, Aylward, in his weakness, wept for a moment. And he thought with fierce joy: Who says I can't understand their language?

Whether his judgment was warped by rage and frustration, or because he saw danger in being so far from his own base at night, the Red commander attacked before it was fully dark. And — Aylward thought — perhaps because of a combination of rage and fear, the Reds did not attack cleverly, taking advantage of the fading light, but instead came in a desperate, surging rush.

Aylward propped himself firmly against the rampart and worked his carbine. He shot at the brief flowering of a rifle flash, at the stirring shadows, at the night moving with grotesque shapes. He fired with furious calm, and when he pressed the magazine release button and his last empty magazine clattered on the rocks, he reversed his hold, grasping the warm barrel in his right hand, swinging the butt at the dark shapes that were leaping at the barrier, screaming in hoarse triumph, bayonets bared.

He thought it was some trick of the eye, some soothing mirage beneficently vouchsafed to a man a single second away from death, when the charging figures faltered and then started to fade away from the barrier, some of them crumpling in their tracks, some of them skidding back down the slope. And then, above his own voice, above the insane howl of his men, he heard another sound, a familiar one, like the voice of a forgotten friend, and he recognized it as the determined chatter of the LMG, .30 caliber.

The rescue party consisted of two squads of the first platoon of Able Company, with Lieutenant Pahlman in command.

Pahlman, leaning over Aylward, whispered, "The Old Man is burning. He figured you got lost. Wait'll we tell him." His teeth gleamed in the darkness as he grinned.

They were busy making improvised litters out of shelter halves and rifles for him and for Gillis and Ostermuller. Szymanowski and Wilson had concluded, contemptuously, that they preferred walking to placing themselves in the hands of raw, untried rookies. Aylward lay quietly on a raincoat, pushing his pain away from him, looking up at the stars, glinting like bright coins in the velvet sky. Then he became aware that he was being lifted and was down again on a litter. He saw a man bend down to grasp the rifle ends and straighten up again as two new shapes loomed up in the darkness. From their voices, which were loud and truculent, he recognized Piccone and Marchese. Then Wilson and Szymanowski chimed in, and there was a general uproar.

Lieutenant Pahlman's stocky figure came into view.

"Now what's this all about?" Pahlman said.

Marchese's voice rose out of the hubbub and established itself with authority. "Look, Lieutenant, I don't want none of them butterfingers carrying this stretcher. Me and Mario will take it."

"You're both pooped," Pahlman said reasonably. "These men are fresh and capable of —"

"Over my dead body," Marchese said decisively. "Right, Mario?"

Lieutenant Pahlman, sensibly taking cognizance of the strain they had been under, continued to be patient with Marchese and Piccone. Aylward, lifting his head with great effort, could see two litters being borne gently down the slope: Gillis and Ostermuller. He shut his eyes, almost comfortably, but they opened again when he heard Marchese going on. Marchese was quite out of hand. He was regaling Pahlman with his personal, *highly* personal, opinion of the first platoon and of the first platoon's crummy lieutenant. He would be blanked if he was going to take orders from any green lieutenant without combat experience (Aylward heard Pahlman, who had been shot at from one bloody end of Korea to the other, sputter like an overchoked engine) who better learn pronto that when he came up against a couple of tough, experienced line soldiers like him and his pal Mario . . .

Pahlman stopped sputtering and began to roar: "Shut up! I'm giving the orders around here! Now get down that slope, or —"

Aylward saw Marchese's Renaissance profile, silhouetted in the faint glow of the moon, close in against Pahlman's so that the tips of their noses seemed to be touching. Piccone, Wilson and Szymanowski stood beside him in a tense, determined group.

Pahlman bellowed, "Peters! Cohen! Pick up that stretcher!"

"Pick it up," Marchese said agreeably. "Pick it up, you guys, and you'll win a bust in the mouth. Nobody but me and Mario carries that stretcher."

Aylward acted quickly to head off the explosion. He raised himself painfully on one elbow and called hoarsely: "Lieutenant Pahlman. Dick." Pahlman's face, contorted with anger, came down into view.

"Dick," Aylward said. "Dick, what's your time in grade?"

Pahlman's mouth dropped open. "Eleven August, Fifty, but —"

"Twenty-eight June, same year," Aylward whispered. "I rank you by a month and a half." He tried to sharpen his wheezing voice to a tone of command. "Private Marchese. Sergeant Piccone. Pick up the litter and move on out. Those are orders, Lieutenant Pahlman."

Marchese lifted the front end of the litter and Piccone the rear, and they started down the rock-strewn slope. Piccone issued instructions. "Don't do like that, Marchese. Take short steps. Bend your knees."

"Get lost, Piccone," Marchese said irritably. He was still for a moment, and then his voice rose on a note of quavering horror. "Hey! I take it back. For God's sake, Mario, *don't* get lost!"

Wilson and Szymanowski, marching to the right and left of the litter (like honor guards in a royal processional, Aylward thought), burst into raucous laughter; and far down the slope, Aylward heard a weak echo of it from Ostermuller and Gillis. After a moment, he grinned.

He saw Lieutenant Pahlman, waiting at the bottom of the cleft, and he gestured to him. Pahlman fell in step alongside the litter, his face brooding and perplexed.

"Sorry to go chicken on you, Dick," Aylward whispered.

Pahlman grunted, mollified, and Aylward thought he detected a note of wistfulness in his voice: "You guys sure do stick by your own."

Aylward was silent as they came down to the flat and started southward toward the culvert, and beyond it, to the sparse farmlands they had traversed a million years ago. Then he cleared his raw throat. "I'll tell you something, Dick," he said confidentially. "Those men happen to be the best six in the best squad in the best platoon —"

"Cornball!" It was Marchese's voice, husky and whispered. "What a cornball!"

Pahlman drifted away. There was no sound as they skirted the culvert, except for the rasp of boots on the dusty earth. Aylward shut his eyes.

"Shimmy!" It was Marchese's voice once again. "Shimmy, lift up your feet! What kind of a way is that to march? You're a disgrace to me and the lieutenant!" He swore savagely, then said: "From now on, you guys better learn to do things right, or you'll have to get out of the squad. Right, Lieutenant?"

"Right," Aylward said, and smiled and looked up at the friendly stars.

The Enemy Beach

by William Chamberlain

THE LCVP — Landing Craft, Vehicles and Personnel — rolled gently in the moderate swell as the afternoon died. Five miles away through the haze the mountains were dirty against the sky, and heat hung over the water like a felt blanket. There was no breeze. Twenty-three men were in the LCVP, and they sat or lay, according to their inclinations, and talked in bored voices.

That was Korea over there. To most of them, Korea was just another place and the job at hand was just another job. As soon as it got dark enough, they would run in to that dim shore line and some of them would go ashore. There was a bridge to be blown up. After they had done that, they would come back. Probably all of them. The possibility that some of them might *not* come back didn't worry them right now because that was something in the future, and it was too hot to worry about something that was in the future.

Twenty of the twenty-three were soldiers. They wore drab fatigues and helmets, and their faces were darkened with burnt cork or old crankcase oil or whatever else had come handy before they had boarded the LCVP. A sergeant was in command and he lounged aft beside the skipper of the craft and made desultory and belittling conversation. His name was MacInnis — a bored man who had seen battle before.

"Mighty soft," he said. "I got to admire you, bud, for pickin' the Navy to fight this war in. Mighty soft."

"Yeah," the skipper said absently. He was worrying a little. It was too hot and still, and there was a black bank of clouds making up over there above the mountains. That could spell nasty weather.

"Mighty soft," Sergeant MacInnis said again.

The skipper's name was Moreland and he was a boatswain's mate, second class. He had curly hair, burned to the color of straw by the sun, and pale eyes and a sensitive face. He was barefooted and twenty-two, and he had been in the Navy for three years. Things worried him. Now he was worried about putting the sergeant and his men on shore. And he was worried about the storm which was blowing up. And he was worried about picking the sergeant and his men up again and taking them back to where he had got them.

Sergeant MacInnis spat over the side of the LCVP. "If I would have had any sense I would have gone in the Navy," he said reflectively. "Nice, cozy bunk to sleep in every night. Good chow. Ain't that right, bud?"

"Sure," Moreland said absently again. There was no wind, but the swells were getting bigger, so that they slapped spray into the LCVP now and then. Back at the ship there had been some scuttlebutt going around about the Reds having a couple of gunboats prowling the coast. That was something else to worry about.

"Now, you take me," Sergeant MacInnis was saying in an aggrieved voice. "What do I get in the Army? Mud in the puss. That's what I get. Mud in the puss."

A corporal, balancing himself against the roll, came aft. He was a chunky youth with a snub nose and cheeks that were peeling. "It makes you look better," he said.

"What makes me look better?" MacInnis wanted to know.

"Mud in the puss," the corporal told him. "Why don't we get going and get this business over with?"

"They told me to put you guys ashore at twenty-one hundred," Moreland said. "That's an hour and a half yet."

"Just like the Navy," the corporal said, squatting down against the side of the LCVP. "Everything by the clock. I bet you even scratch by the clock, don't you?"

Moreland looked at him a little vaguely. "Naw," he said, "we don't do that. . . . You sure you got those flares to signal with when you want me to pick you up, Sergeant?"

"Aw, don't worry about that, bud," Sergeant Mac-Innis told him. "The Army's always got flares. We don't need no flares. We'll burn a house down. Maybe two houses."

"Yeah," the corporal said. "Then the big wheels will burn you. Didn't you know that this is a civilized war?"

"I didn't know that it was a war, period," Sergeant MacInnis said. "I thought we just come out here on a police job."

"A dummy," the corporal said without rancor, banging a heel up and down against the deck. "A big, ignorant dummy with chevrons on, an' I got to trust my life to him. I bet my mother wouldn't like it if she knew."

"I bet you never had a mother," Sergeant MacInnis said. "I bet they found you under a beer keg."

Moreland wasn't paying any attention. He looked at his watch for the fiftieth time, and then looked at those clouds over the mountains again. His crew — a motor machinist's mate, second class, named Ed, and a seaman — sat on the engine hatch and gossiped idly about the merits of the girls in Japan. Moreland suddenly felt very much alone. It seemed to him that he was the only one of the whole twenty-three who felt any responsibility for this affair.

The thought increased that rat's-gnaw of worry in him. They ought to start in pretty soon — maybe forty minutes or so. The clouds had got blacker and the day was almost gone. He mopped his face and eased the wheel to meet a big swell, and then beckoned to the seaman sitting on the engine hatch.

"Hey, Ostrowski," he said, "take over for a little, will you? I want to have another look." Ostrowski hunched himself across the hatch.

Ed, the motor mach, said, "You'll wear that beach out, lookin'." He was a big, solid man with black hair which kept falling down into his eyes. He and Moreland had been together for two years now. They neither liked nor disliked each other. Ostrowski had just come out a month ago. Moreland didn't know him very well.

"I like to be sure about things," Moreland said.

"Okay. Okay," Ed said. "It's your party."

That was the trouble, Moreland thought a little resentfully. That was what everybody figured: it was his party. Sergeant MacInnis, the corporal, Ed, Ostrowski — the whole bunch of them. They just sat on their duffs and figured it was his party.

In spite of the dim light, the glasses brought the beach up close to him. Not much of a beach. Maybe a hundred yards of shingle where a stream came down out of the hills. The soldiers would go up that stream until they came to the railway bridge. That was the way he understood it. Then they would blow the bridge and come back. Nothing to it. That was what they had told him at the ship. Absolutely nothing to it. Nothing to it, he thought sourly, if that storm didn't come whooping down, and if he didn't run into any Red gunboats, and if he didn't run this bucket onto the rocks trying to find the beach again in the dark. He put the glasses away and fished for a cigarette.

Sergeant MacInnis had gone forward, but he came back now, stepping over the legs of soldiers sprawled in the bottom of the LCVP. "Hey, bud," he said, "when do we go?"

"Pretty soon now," Moreland told him. "Look, we can't sit there on the beach and wait for you guys to come back. We got to pull out again as soon as we land you. We'll wait offshore until we get your signal. You got that straight?"

"Sure, sure," MacInnis said impatiently. "Don't get yourself in an uproar. The Army'll handle things okay."

Ostrowski laughed raucously at that. "Yeah," he said, "they'll handle things okay. I remember one time . . ."

Sergeant MacInnis scowled. Now that it was about time to go in, he was getting a little edgy himself. "Never mind about one time, pal," he said darkly. "You just steer this scow an' leave the Army out of it. . . . How long is *pretty soon?*" he asked Moreland.

"Twenty minutes," Moreland said.

MacInnis grunted and shouted to his men to check their equipment again. Then he leaned his arms on the gunwale and spat moodily into the darkening sea. "Yes, sir," he said, "I sure should of gone into the Navy. While I'm beatin' my brains out up in that lousy valley, what'll you be doin'? Cruisin' around in a nice, comfortable boat. That's what you'll be doin'."

Moreland didn't say anything.

"Takin' life easy," Sergeant MacInnis went on. "That's the Navy for you. Whenever there's a nasty job to be done, do they send for the Navy? Not much, they don't. They send for the poor, dumb dogfaces. The Navy sets back an' takes five."

Ostrowski, at the wheel, made rude sounds with his mouth. "What you gripin' about, Mac?" he wanted to know. "We brought you here an' we'll take you back. What you want for your nickel?"

"Not what I got," Sergeant MacInnis said sadly.

The darkness was coming down fast now. Across the water, the mountains were growing dim against the sullen thunderheads and the evening seemed to get hotter. Once a dull glow of lightning, very far away, washed across the sky. Moreland looked at his watch again.

"Time to go," he said.

He took the wheel and straightened the LCVP away, and the engine racketed noisily as they headed toward the beach. The rollers were bigger and more oily now. The boat didn't handle right, Moreland thought. He had been thinking that all the way up the coast. It handled like a log in the water and the engine missed now and then.

The corporal came back to stand by Sergeant Mac-Innis. "How we goin' to work it, Pete?" he asked.

"Work what?" MacInnis said peevishly.

"Goin' up the valley."

"Same as we always have," Sergeant MacInnis said, irritation quickening his voice. "Same as any other patrol. What did you think we were going to do? Form up in a column of doodads like we was paradin' down Broadway? Get some sense."

The LCVP dug its nose into the rollers now and then, slapping down hard so that spray came over the bow. A soldier swore petulantly as he wiped off his dripping carbine. They'd reach the beach in another ten minutes, Moreland thought. He hoped that there weren't any rocks in the cove where the stream came

out of the hills. Probably were, though. That was the
way his luck had been running lately.

As they got closer, the beach seemed to come at
him with a terrific speed. He was sure that there were
rocks now. He wondered if he ought to turn around
and go back to the ship and tell them that there were
too many rocks to land safely. They wouldn't like
that. He'd get chewed out good.

He told Ostrowski to go forward and tend the
ramp. Ed was fiddling with the engine — it was still
missing and Moreland worried about that. Sergeant
MacInnis was giving last-minute instructions to his
men, yelling to make himself heard above the racket
of the engine. The mountains seemed to hang over
them now, and Moreland had the uneasy feeling that
eyes were watching them come in.

"If any of you get separated from the rest, work
back to the beach an' wait there," Sergeant MacInnis
was saying.

A man asked, "Suppose a guy gets wounded?"

"Don't get wounded," Sergeant MacInnis said petulantly. "You ain't paid to get wounded."

The surf on the beach was heavier than he had
figured, Moreland thought. Well, he'd shove in hard
anyway. He didn't want to dump the soldiers off in

swimming water. They were about a hundred yards out and it was so dark that he could see little but the black bulk of the mountains and the white line that the water made where it ran up onto the shingle. He headed the boat toward the mid-point of that line and hoped that everything was going to be all right. He didn't think it was.

"Hang on!" he yelled to the soldiers. "This is it!"

He felt the bow lift as it struck the shelving beach and the boat bucked forward until it finally stuck. He could see the vague silhouettes of the soldiers as they moved forward.

For a moment he was glad that he was in the Navy. He wondered how he would feel if he were one of those guys walking out there into the blackness; leaving the safety of the boat for the uncertainties of the dark land. He thought of them fumbling their way up the valley and he thought of the Red patrols that were probably prowling around up there too. Sergeant MacInnis was probably right, he guessed. The Navy did have it pretty good.

MacInnis called back to him, "Maybe we'll come out of here in a hurry, bud! You come quick when we signal, huh?"

"Sure," Moreland said. "We'll be right here."

The night swallowed him, and Ostrowski's voice came back, "They're all ashore, Steve. Wind the ramp up?"

"Wind her up," Moreland said.

He heard the clank of the winch dogs and then Ostrowski yelled, "Take her away!" and he reversed the engine. The boat shuddered and then an incoming roller lifted it and broke it loose from the shingle and they backed out into the surf again. Ostrowski came aft and leaned against the engine hatch.

"You know what I'm goin' to do when I get back to the States?" he asked of nobody in particular. "I'm goin' to buy me a farm out in the middle of Kansas where there ain't no water. The most water I'm ever goin' to get close to again will be in a bathtub."

Moreland didn't answer. The boat was fifty yards from the beach now, and he reversed his engine again and cautiously started his turn. The boat responded sluggishly, plodding around like a blind old man tapping with his cane. Moreland was suddenly worried for fear he hadn't allowed himself enough sea room for the turn; halfway around, the LCVP faltered and hung broadside to the rollers which were rushing toward the beach. For a sickening moment he had the feeling that they were going to capsize.

The engine coughed asthmatically again, and Ed, still fiddling with it, swore, and the sweat began to come out on Moreland's face. They were drifting back toward the beach. He pushed desperately at the wheel, trying to pull the blunt bow around by main strength. Then, after a long time, the boat came around and they were headed out to sea again, and the beach was falling behind.

"A bathtub," Ostrowski said again. "That'll be enough water for Mrs. Ostrowski's little boy."

Moreland wiped his face. He wondered what he would have done if they had broached to, back there in the surf. That would have been a hell of a thing. Sergeant MacInnis could have signaled until he was blue in the face for all the good it would have done him. You didn't get a landing craft off once it had gone broadside onto a beach.

The heat became more oppressive and it hung around Moreland's neck like a soggy gunnysack. The engine still coughed, but it kept going and presently they were two thousand yards out. Moreland throttled back and allowed the boat to drift. It lost headway at once and slid into the trough, and that was no good. There was too much of a sea running. He advanced the throttle again, running just fast enough to keep steerageway, and headed on out to sea. Ed straightened up slowly from where he had been squatting on the other side of the engine hatch.

"What's the trouble?" Moreland asked. A capful of wind cooled his face. Again there was that faint and faraway flicker of lightning against the black wall of the clouds.

"Injector, I think," Ed said morosely.

"Can you fix it?"

"Have to tear it down." Ed looked at the lowering clouds. "Wouldn't be no good if a squall would hit us."

The thread of worry became stronger in Moreland. "Maybe it'll be all right. I guess we better take a chance on it."

Ed leaned against the engine hatch and stared moodily back to where the white line of the surf was thinning against the blackness of the mountains.

"It's a crummy war," he said. "What'd you go into the Navy for, Steve?"

"I was too young to get into the last war and I wanted to see what it was like," Moreland told him. "Both my brothers were in the last one and they used to kid me. So I enlisted."

Ed grunted. "Boy, you got it comin' to you, then. I'd still be playin' pool in Jerry Eckert's place back in Sioux City if the draft board hadn't started breathin' down my neck. I figured I'd rather be in the Navy than puttin' one foot ahead of the other in the infantry." He paused and spat over the side. "I'm lucky, at that, I guess. Look at them poor buzzardly doughfoots goin' up that valley tonight."

"Yeah," Moreland said. "They got it rugged."

Ed went forward to join Ostrowski, who was leaning on the gunwale staring off into the darkness. Moreland was glad that Ed was gone. He didn't want to talk right now. The memory of what Sergeant MacInnis had said still bothered him. After all, it *was* pretty soft to take it easy out here while those guys were slugging it out up there in the valley. It worried him a little.

Then Ostrowski called softly, "Look over there to port, Steve."

Moreland started and strained his eyes.

There was still a little starlight off in that direction where the clouds hadn't come down yet. He saw it, then — a sinister, squat shape which loomed vaguely on the crest of a roller, and then sank back out of sight again. Ostrowski came back, balancing against the heave of the deck.

"Take her," Moreland said, and reached for the glasses.

"You think it's that condemned gunboat?"

"Maybe," Moreland said.

The powerful glasses brought the dark shape of the other craft up close. It was wicked-looking — a couple of miles away and plowing along on a collision course with the LCVP. He couldn't be sure, but Moreland thought that he could make out the shape of a gun on her forward deck. It was a Red gunboat, all right, he thought. He had never seen a silhouette like that before.

Ed came aft, voice worried, "One of theirs, Steve?"

"Yeah, I think so."

"And us without so much as a machine gun," Ed said bitterly. "What are we supposed to do? Throw rocks?"

"Take it easy," Moreland told him.

He didn't feel easy.

He took the wheel again and swung the boat around, taking a beating in the trough again as he headed back toward the beach. They were low in the water; maybe the gunboat wouldn't spot them. Anyway, it was all that he could do. Ed and Ostrowski were quiet.

They wallowed along for five minutes and Moreland saw that the gunboat would pass them to seaward, if they were lucky. He throttled back the engine, hoping that it wouldn't die. The gunboat was close now; and it was better to risk the beating they would take, lying dead in the water, than the racket that the engine made. A sudden gust of wind slapped at his face and then was gone, leaving the night hot and sticky again. The storm would break pretty soon, he thought.

"You figure they see us?" Ostrowski whispered.

Ed answered him irritably, "How do I know? If they start shootin', you can figure they see us, all right."

The boat lurched to the crest of a swell and Moreland saw that the gunboat was dead astern and crossing behind them. He could hear Ed breathing noisily through his open mouth, like a man at the end of a long run.

Someone called out on the deck of the gunboat — a shrill jabbering which carried clearly in the hot night.

Then the boat dropped back into the trough again and Moreland drew in his own breath. "We're lucky so far," he said.

When they rolled onto the next crest, the gunboat was three hundred yards to port; Moreland's heart began to crawl back out of his throat. He picked up the glasses and focused them: the gunboat was moving slowly south, apparently unsuspicious.

"Brother," Ostrowski said feelingly, "for a minute I could feel bullets stitchin' right up my back."

Moreland frowned, but didn't say anything. The gunboat was a mile away now, but it was behaving queerly. For a few minutes it slowed as though undecided; then he saw that it was turning to come back on a course which would take it inshore of where they lay. He didn't like that. Another of those gusts of wind — coming as suddenly as the puff of smoke from a cannon — beat at his face.

"The gooks have smelled something," he said under his breath. "They're coming back. We got to run out to sea before they get too close. Baby that engine along, Ed."

Neither Ed nor Ostrowski said anything. They knew well enough that the chips were down; no use to cry about it. The engine stuttered into life and

Moreland brought the bow of the boat back into the sea. The clouds had come down so close now that he thought he could almost touch them, and he wished that the rain would come.

They had just got straightened out when lightning ripped out of the sky to send a flickering blue glow across the water. In that split second Moreland saw the gunboat plainly; guessed that the gunboat had seen them too. Thunder crashed down like the slamming of a bank of giant furnace doors. Another flash came and, in it, Moreland caught a glimpse of Ostrowski crossing himself.

Ed was squatting on the deck listening to the engine. "This ain't our night, Steve," he said. "She's missing worse."

On the gunboat a searchlight winked on, its slim beam probing across the tumbled water. Nothing to do but hang on and hope, Moreland thought. The light touched the beach first and then swung seaward in an arc which was agonizingly slow. The three watched, mutely fascinated, as it came nearer, flicking across the white crests of the seas. It passed over the LCVP — moving hazily — and Moreland could see the faces of his crew limned starkly for a moment.

Ed was chewing gum with a steady up-and-down movement of his heavy jaws. Ostrowski was whistling, his lips puckered up stiffly. Moreland's own face felt pinched and tight. He was scared. He had never been more scared in his life. Abstractedly, he wondered if his brothers had been scared at Leyte Gulf and the Coral Sea.

The light went on ahead for a mile. Then it came crawling back and stopped squarely on them. The gunboat was closing fast. A cannon began to fire with a sharp *Pom . . . pom . . . pom*, its flashes winking across the water. Twenty-millimeter, Moreland thought with a vague detachment. That was what it sounded like. He could see the splashes walking up the searchlight beam toward them.

"Get down!" he yelled to Ostrowski and Ed.

Then he thought, That was silly. One of those 20-mm. shells would probably go through the thin skin of the boat like an icepick through tissue paper. . . . He didn't know. . . .

Something slapped amidships like a hammer striking an anvil, and there was a nasty flash and he heard the whine of bits of metal. Then the boat fell off into the trough, and the sea hid the gunboat for a moment. Moreland was grateful for that. As they lifted to the crest of the next wave, the squall came — breaking with a howling fury. Moreland let out his breath again. A beautiful, beautiful squall.

It whooped down like a hawk diving on a chicken. One moment the sea had been clear, with the search-light slicing across it like a silver knife. The next moment there was nothing there but a solid gray wall of rain driving in horizontal sheets. The wind came in like a solid fist, beating Moreland against the wheel and holding him there with a giant hand against his back. An eerie wailing filled the night as the gale skated across the gunwales.

Ed crawled forward; came crawling back to haul himself up beside Moreland and yell in his ear: "We got a hole in us! Big as a cantaloupe an' down low! We're takin' water!"

"Tend the wheel!" Moreland yelled back.

He got a battle lantern and a couple of life jackets that had been discarded by the soldiers, and crawled forward. Ostrowski was there, back to the rain that was driving the length of the boat. Water was slosh-ing about on the deck and the battle lantern showed Moreland the jagged hole.

"Hold the lantern!" he yelled to Ostrowski.

Working carefully, he wadded up a life jacket and

shoved it into the hole as a plug. A driving sea slapped
it back into his stomach. He tried again. No luck.
The third time it stayed long enough for him to punch
it tight. Maybe it would stay, he thought; maybe it
wouldn't. Anyway, it was all he could do.

"Stay and watch it," he told Ostrowski, and went
aft again.

The rain struck him like the stream from a fire
hose as he pulled himself up by the engine hatch.
Driven by the wind, the boat was scudding violently
ahead into a blank wall, and, as Moreland took the
wheel, he had the trapped sensation of a man walking
in the dark in a strange room. He had the feeling that
there was something just ahead beyond that gray curtain and that they were about to crash into it headlong. The impulse to put the wheel over to avoid it
was almost overpowering, but he fought it down and
held the boat steady.

They went on. They were getting too far out to
sea, he knew, but he was afraid to try to turn in the
face of that wind. It seemed to him that they were
racing at tremendous speed. The boat would race to
the top of a sea, its bow climbing at a steep angle; then
dive down the other side like a runaway car on a

roller coaster. Salt spray came back with the rain to sting his lips.

The luminous dial of his watch said that it was twenty-three-thirty, and that shocked him. He hadn't realized that so much time had gone. He'd have to turn, wind or no wind. Sergeant MacInnis and his men might be waiting back there on the beach right now. He reached out and nudged Ed with his toe.

"Got to turn!" he shouted. "Give me a hand with the wheel! It's going to be rough!"

No use being finicky about it, he thought. Get it over with . . . either they'd make it or they wouldn't. Ed shouldered up beside him and put hands on the wheel. The rudder fought them violently, but they got it over, and the boat began to swing with slow reluctance.

It was three-quarters broadside to the sea when the engine died. The stopping of its racket bit into Moreland's consciousness like a sudden shower of icy needles. This was going to be bad.

"For God's sake, get it started again!" he yelled at Ed, but Ed was already on his knees, getting the side cover off the engine hatch.

"Lantern!" Ed yelled back at him.

They fell off broadside into the trough as Moreland

crawled forward to where Ostrowski was. A sea bigger than the rest stood the boat almost on its beamends and pitched Moreland against the side. The gunwale raked the skin from his bare shoulder and the impact made him dizzy. He crawled on to where Ostrowski was, and got the battle lantern and crawled aft again with Ostrowski following him.

"Get the cover off the other side of the hatch!" Ed yelled. "I got to get in there in a minute!"

Moreland passed the battle lantern to Ostrowski again. "Hold it for him. I'll take care of the cover."

He had to be doing something. The boat was lying like a log in the water now, and every time they fell off into the trough he thought they were going over. Bracing himself against the side, he fumbled at the cover. It came loose finally. Then they fell off into a trough deeper than the rest and the boat heeled far over — so far that Moreland sucked in his breath involuntarily.

He shoved out his left hand to keep from going over the engine hatch, and pain suddenly raced up his arm like the stab of a knife. He had jammed his palm against the exhaust, which was almost red-hot. Shock flattened him on the deck for a moment; then he managed to sit up again. Across the hatch he could hear Ed swearing.

"Curse all engines!" Ed was saying. "Curse all engines!"

He could hear Ed's voice very clearly, and that puzzled him for a moment. There was something wrong in that. Then he realized what it was. The wind had gone as suddenly as it had come, and the rain was a sullen drip instead of a wall of water blasting across the sea. The squall had passed on over them, and the sudden quietness, after the roaring tumult of the last two hours, was like an ache.

Moreland's left arm was a solid chunk of pain. He touched the palm of his hand with his fingers and knew that it was not good; then, holding the hand up, he crawled back to where the first-aid kit was stowed. Working by touch in the darkness, he smeared petroleum jelly over the burn and wrapped his hand clumsily in gauze, tying the knot with his other hand and his teeth. Then he got back to the wheel and clung there and watched Ed and Ostrowski working in the dull glow of the battle lantern.

The time was zero one hundred.

Ostrowski said, his voice worried, "We got to pick

them guys up. It would be a heck of a thing to leave 'em on the beach."

Ed grunted and said nothing. It seemed like a long while later when he called to Moreland, "Try her, Steve."

Moreland tried. Tried some more. Then, after a million years, the engine caught, stuttered twice and then settled down into a steady racket. It sounded awful sweet to Steve Moreland. Ostrowski came to help him with the wheel and, almost imperceptibly at first, the boat began to gather headway. They took a beating, quartering to the sea, and then they were headed back toward the beach.

Still rugged, though. The following seas caught up with them and came over the stern and battered them with green water. It was going to be bad on the beach, Moreland thought. That worried him now. The rain stopped and the clouds were beginning to break, and there was a dull glow where a moon was trying to come through. That worried him too. What if that gunboat was still around?

The engine was running well, and Ed came to stand by the wheel. "What's the matter with your hand?" he asked.

"Burned it," Moreland said briefly. He didn't want to talk about it.

"Better let me take the wheel," Ed said. "It's bad to burn your hand."

"It's all right," Moreland told him. "Just scorched a little." That was a lie. It was cooked like a steak, but it was his job to run this tub.

The moon came through finally, washing the sea with white light as though it wanted to make up for the pitchy blackness that had gone before. The waters around them were empty, and Moreland grunted with relief. At least they had got rid of that gunboat. Miles away, the mountains were stark and grim.

They went on. They were less than a mile out when Ostrowski said, "There it is," and Moreland saw a white flare shoot up from the land dead ahead on the course they were steering. He felt a little flick of pride that they had come back to hit the beach on the nose.

It was rough going in through surf like this. Still, it had to be done. He jammed the boat in hard again and Ostrowski dropped the ramp, and Sergeant MacInnis and his men, stark in the moonlight, poured aboard. Then the ramp was up again and they were backing out through the surf. Moreland gave himself plenty of room for his turn this time, and presently they straightened away for the run back to the ship.

Sergeant MacInnis came aft.

"Rugged," he said tiredly. "Plenty rugged up there."

"You blow the bridge?" Moreland asked him.

"We blew her, bud. But it was rugged. I should have gone in the Navy like you. Nothin' to do but ride around in a boat."

"Yeah," Moreland said. "I guess that's right."

Moreland sat in the operations shack the next morning and looked at the form in front of him. His left hand had been dressed and felt pretty good now. After a moment, he moistened a stub of pencil with his tongue and filled in the date on the form. After that he sat back for a moment, scowling. He was thinking again of what those guys must have felt like . . . going up the valley in the dark. It took a lot of guts to do that.

He shrugged, finally, and bent over the form, moistening his pencil again. In the proper space he wrote *Nothing unusual to report,* and signed his name.

Spy Mission to Inchon

by Emile C. Schurmacher

WATCHING the four sampans approach from enemy-held Taebu-do Island, Lieutenant Eugene Franklin Clark USN chomped expectantly upon the end of a frayed cigar butt and shifted the .45-caliber "grease gun" under his arm.

Plainly Captain Twantze was overeager. The boom of a 37-mm. antitank gun reached Clark's ears as the enemy opened up from the bow of the captain's engine-powered sampan, at a distance of a mile.

The 37-mm. shell geysered the oily calmness of the water a half-mile in front of the bow of Clark's one-sampan navy. Shrill cries of victory already were shredding the Yellow Sea twilight from excited Chinese and North Koreans aboard the three sailing sampans of Twantze's "assault armada."

A bit premature, Clark thought to himself and

glanced upward. Interrupted in their fishing, three gulls had taken off resentfully in the direction of Inchon harbor.

Twantze's 37-mm. spoke again. The second geyser spouted only a trifle closer. At the wheel of Clark's sampan, re-christened *Flagship*, old Soji Iwon waggled his goatlike beard and muttered fiercely.

Clark turned to his interpreter, Assebo-born Sammy Wai. "Tell him there is nothing to fear from the anti-tank gun. Their gunnery is pretty terrible."

There was a rapid exchange in Korean. Then Sammy Wai said in good G.I. English, "Old guy ain't worried about getting clobbered. Thinks we might get snafued in the mud or the one-lunger conk out again."

"*Flagship* draws less than four feet of water," Clark pointed out calmly. "There's ten under the keel right now. As for the engine —" he held up two crossed fingers. The antiquated one-cylinder make-and-break engine was running, mostly on hope.

He glanced around at the other members of the crew to see how they were behaving under fire. There were half a dozen of them. Bright-eyed, adventurous boys between fifteen and eighteen years of age, who grinned back at him cheerfully. They were members of what he jokingly called his "Young Men's Association."

Clark was justly proud of his little seagoing army. Since landing secretly on Yonghung-do, only a week before, he had accomplished wonders with his South Korean boys. He had taught several of them on the island to handle the grenades, "grease guns," and the two fifty-caliber heavy machine guns which had been unloaded with him from a Korean frigate. One of the machine guns was now mounted in the bow of the twenty-five-foot *Flagship*, surrounded by sandbags.

Clark sauntered forward to the fifty-caliber, alertly manned by two of his seventeen-year-olds, Hayjun and Sienso. When he spoke to them they understood his halting Korean much better than did old Soji Iwon.

"Don't get trigger-happy," he warned. "Wait until I order fire and then I'll lend a hand."

They beamed in anticipation. Sienso pointed as a third shell splashed far ahead with a faintly heard *pul-lump*. "Bimeby Twantze have no more shell for boom-boom!"

Clark grinned at Sienso. "Maybe," he said. "But let's not count on it."

By this time the engine-powered enemy sampan

was pulling well ahead of the three sailers. Above the yells of victory, Twantze's voice could be heard. He sounded like a yapping mongrel as he angrily gave new orders to his gun crew. The flustered gunners responded by elevating the muzzle of the 37-mm. A shell screeched high over Clark's head, speeding in the general direction of South China. *Flagship* stuck doggedly to her course without returning fire. At a distance of two hundred yards, Clark came forward again and squatted down behind the machine gun with Hayjun and Sienso.

Another fifty yards and Captain Twantze's overtightened nerves snapped. He was chagrined at the failure of his gun crew to register a hit. He was disturbed by the ominous silence of the approaching enemy and the deliberate impudence with which *Flagship* had thrust herself into point-blank range. Moreover, he suspected that there was something even more lethal aboard her than the fifty-caliber machine gun, whose muzzle eyed him balefully over the top of the sandbags. Some terrible secret weapon . . .

Twantze scrambled to the stern of his boat and shouted to the riflemen on the sailers behind to open fire. They sounded off with a ragged volley like the exploding of a carelessly put together string of fire-crackers. Another volley . . . A few bullets thudded harmlessly into *Flagship*'s squat hull.

At a range of one hundred yards Clark nodded his Navy-bill-capped head. "All right. Let's give it to 'em!"

The machine gun opened fire with deadly effective-ness. As the first burst hammered home, Twantze decided it was enough. This was not his idea of fighting. Jumping off the stern, he began swimming back towards Taebu-do with frantic strokes. Thus he alone escaped the starkly brief massacre on the first sampan.

At point-blank range Clark and his two boys stitched the sampan with an extra burst along the waterline. The sea poured through her hull as if she were an old washtub, and she sank rapidly. The reac-tion to this aboard the three sailers, still several hun-dred yards behind her, was complete panic. The crews tried to put about and flee. The riflemen fired wildly, screaming for them to hurry.

Ominously, *Flagship* chugged onward toward the nearest sailer, catching her neatly as she tried to put about. Four men jumped overboard before the machine gun opened fire again. The others died in a withering hail of bullets. The sailer began to sink.

Clark pointed to one of the two remaining sailers and sang out a command. Old Soji Iwon's goat beard waggled with excitement while he spun the wheel. This time he needed neither encouragement nor an interpreter. *Flagship* chugged valiantly forward for ten yards. And then, for the fifteenth or sixteenth time that day, her temperamental one-lunger died.

With a sigh of resignation Clark approached the formidable flywheel. He took a familiar stance, ankle-deep in oily bilge, reaching for a handy wrench. When he looked up again after coaxing the engine back to life, the two remaining enemy sailers had escaped and were nearing Taebu-do.

"One of 'em picked up Twantze while you were working on the engine, Lieutenant," Sammy Wai reported ruefully. "I made a couple of tries with my carbine. No good."

"No matter," Clark answered, glancing over the water. "Stand by to receive visitors."

Three half-drowned survivors of the sailer were still treading water in various stages of exhaustion. With the aid of a ten-foot bamboo sounding pole,

Sammy Wai and some of the boys hauled them aboard.

A cheering reception committee was waiting for Clark on the muddy bank when *Flagship* chugged back to Yonghung-do. Fully a score of members of his Young Men's Association were there, all carrying small arms. At their head was an older man, "Two-gun Joe," with two .45's tucked in the waistband of his old army fatigues. Joe, like Sammy Wai, was an interpreter Clark had brought to the island with him. He was short and tough, solidly built as a Nagano house, an excellent soldier.

"Take charge of the prisoners," Clark told Joe. "Bring 'em up to H.Q. one at a time. Usual interrogation."

Joe grunted and herded the three cowed prisoners together. He dropped his hands threateningly to the butts of his .45's. "Whenever you're ready, Lieutenant."

Clark's headquarters, a few hundred yards from the water edge, was an eight-man tent which had been unloaded from the Korean frigate with the other supplies. It contained three cots, a folding table on which a small but powerful two-way radio had been set up, and the sparse gear of Clark and the two interpreters. It had also, briefly, accommodated another occupant, a small but deadly green-and-orange species of coral snake which had crawled into Clark's sea bag. On the morning following his landing on Yonghung-do, Clark had reached towards the bag, intent on breaking out some C ration. He had withdrawn his hand just in time, grabbed up his .45 and killed the snake.

Flanked by a guard of armed boys, Joe brought the prisoners to H.Q. Sammy questioned the first two. They were frightened North Korean farmers, less than a week removed from the rice paddies. They explained that the Communists had shoved rifles in their hands, shown them how to load, point the guns and pull triggers. Then they were told that they were soldiers and bundled off to Inchon.

The third prisoner, a Chinese, Lu Pai Chang, aroused Clark's interest. He took over the interrogation when Chang readily admitted that until a few days before he had been one of hundreds of laborers strengthening the defenses of the island fortress of Wolmi-do, "Moon-tip Island," which was connected to the Inchon mainland by a stone causeway.

"This island has cannon?" Clark asked.

"Many monster cannon, numbering twice the number of fingers on my two hands," Chang disclosed. "We poured much concrete around them. We also built tunnels and trenches leading from one to the other."

Clark probed further. From the prisoner's answers he gathered that there were at least a thousand troops massed in the fortress commanding the harbor entrance to Inchon, and that the entire island was honeycombed with tunnels and passages.

Later that night, he coded his daily collection of information to send his intelligence report to Tokyo.

Report seaward side Wolmi-do. . . . Twenty repeat twenty . . . heavy coastal defense guns . . . imperative to silence . . . before assault Red and Blue beaches. . . .

Lieutenant Clark was winding up another busy day. On Yonghung-do, less than ten miles from Inchon and literally under the enemy's nose, he was sending another complete and accurate report to Major General Oliver P. Smith USMC and Rear Admiral James H. Doyle, who were preparing the master plan for the Inchon landing.

The success or failure of an assault on Inchon depended a great deal on Lieutenant Clark and his Top Secret assignment.

Back in August, the U. N. High Command had decided it was vital to take Inchon, and as quickly as possible. D-day had been set for September 15. Considering that almost nine months went into the planning of the Guadalcanal assault in World War II, twenty-three days to get ready for Inchon seemed a fantastic impossibility.

Inchon was a strongly fortified bastion which the Communists believed impregnable. The U. N. High Command knew that its approach was guarded not only by Wolmi-do but by tremendous tides, a tricky channel, mud flats, seawalls and any number of other obstacles and traps. But specific information was lacking. Before a master plan could be evolved, this information must be obtained.

So Lieutenant Clark had been entrusted with a daring spy mission. Square-jawed, dark-haired and broad-shouldered, Clark was a veteran of many South Pacific campaigns in World War II. He had been an officer on U.S.S. *Arneb* and commanded an LST afterwards. He spoke Japanese, Chinese, and a smattering of Korean.

"You have two weeks to find out all you can," he was told. "The mission, of course, is Top Secret. Report to Rear Admiral William G. Andrewes, Royal Navy, in Sasebo. He has been briefed."

Admiral Andrewes commanded the war vessels on patrol in the Yellow Sea off the west coast of Korea. He had put Clark, his two interpreters and supplies on H.M.S. *Charity*, on the night of August 30.

The following morning Andrewes shared the all-important secret with Commander Lee of the ROK Navy. Lee was cruising in the Yellow Sea on his small frigate, *PC-703*. Andrewes wirelessed him orders to meet H.M.S. *Charity* thirty miles off Inchon, in the vicinity of Tokchok Island. To avoid enemy suspicion, it was best not to take the British destroyer any closer to Inchon. Early on the morning of September 1, the two ships had their rendezvous. Clark and his little outfit were transferred aboard *PC-703*. The tiny frigate sailed towards the rocky island of Yonghung-do, at the mouth of the ship channel to Inchon. A mile from the island, the ROK Navy officer cut his engine.

"Now we wait," he informed Clark. "The fishing sampans should be putting out before long."

"How do they feel about us on Yonghung-do?" Clark asked.

"Friendly — I think. Fishing village."

Clark nodded thoughtfully. . . . Lee wasn't sure; no one was sure of anything about this part of enemy-held Korea.

Clark's speculative glance wandered towards Tae-bu-do, silhouetted against the morning sun a few miles to the right. Lee answered his unspoken question.

"Enemy-held. Understand there's a Captain Twantze in command, and he's out to make a name for himself."

A little while later, as Lee had predicted, a fishing sampan chugged cockily across the frigate's bow. It was the only engine-powered boat that Yonghung-do boasted, and old Soji Iwon was at the wheel. Lee hailed him. At high noon on September 1, Lieutenant Clark, Sammy and Joe had landed on Yonghung-do. They carried their .45's in easy reach. In addition, Clark carried a grenade in the pocket of his Marine fatigue greens. Day and night the grenade was to be with him. It was, as he said, his "insurance policy."

Clark had made up his mind to use the grenade on himself if threatened with capture. He had heard many unpleasant stories about the ingenuity and skill of the enemy in torturing prisoners to extract information. And he was determined that under no condition would the secret of the impending invasion of Inchon be wrested from him. As for Sam and Joe, while they might suspect the reason for the mission, they had been told nothing about the imminence of D-day.

As the supplies were unloaded on the shore, boys of all ages flocked around quickly, looking over the military equipment with eager-eyed curiosity. Before long, the Mayor of Yonghung-do, a grizzled Korean named Engsan, appeared from the direction of the village to find out what it was all about.

Clark introduced himself. "I'm Lieutenant Clark, United States Navy," he said matter-of-factly. "I'm setting up my headquarters here."

Engsan looked at Clark and his equipment. His gaze wandered towards the island of Taebu-do, then back to Clark's square-jawed face once more.

"We are peaceful fishermen on Yonghung-do," he declared hesitantly. "We wish no trouble with anyone."

Clark nodded in agreement. "But suppose Twantze decides to bring the trouble to you and you are helpless? We can protect your island."

"Well —"

The cheers of the boys stopped Engsan. It was they who made the decision.

Clark and his two interpreters had gone to work immediately. Before sundown they had set up headquarters and recruited more than one hundred and fifty enthusiastic boys for the Young Men's Association. This was the most bizarre military organization in history, and one of the youngest. It could not properly be termed a guerrilla band. Clark efficiently divided the boys into three groups: the "Army," to guard the island and any prisoners that might be captured; the "Navy," to raid enemy sampans aboard *Flagship*; and, most important of all, the "Intelligence unit" to help gather military information on the mainland.

That first evening, Joe had assembled the Army and Navy and began small-arms instruction. Clark and Sammy had had a session with the Intelligence unit, gratified to find that three of the boys had recently been to Inchon and that one observant sixteen-year-old had been on Wolmi-do.

Shortly before midnight they had set up the radio and Clark had raised Tokyo without trouble. He grinned tiredly.

"Might as well let 'em know we're on the job," he chuckled to Sammy. "Here we go: *Report one seasoned company enemy entrenched behind seawall Inchon tidal basin . . . report fire control tower on Wolmi-do located big red building. . . . We have begun to operate. . . .*"

Not quite twelve hours since Clark had landed on Yonghung-do, he had begun transmitting valuable Intelligence reports.

On the following morning he had assigned missions on the mainland. He had screened ten boys old enough and smart enough to mingle with the natives of Inchon, Seoul and other nearby towns without arousing suspicion. "Keep your eyes and ears open, your mouths closed," he cautioned them. "Take no unnecessary risks." The latter sounded like hollow mockery and he knew it. Every one of the boys was risking his life: death was almost certain if any of them were captured. But there was no alternative. Time was important. It was already less than two weeks to D-day and there was a vast amount of information to be gathered.

He had selected boys to go to Inchon, Seoul, Wolmi-do, the Kimpo airfield — carefully explaining to them what they were to observe. When they had set out in fishing sampans and in rowboats, Clark saw them off with a tugging at his heart.

"Here's hoping they all come back," he muttered to Sammy. Then — "Let's get on with the job."

Soji Iwon's engine-powered sampan was quickly activated for the Yonghung-do Navy, and a fifty-caliber machine gun mounted in the bow. On September 3 *Flagship* was then ready for her first raid. And now, under Clark's command, she had chugged out into the ship channel and, in the course of the exciting day, captured four enemy sampans from Inchon. It was very gratifying.

The prisoners, sixteen in all, were taken back to Yonghung-do for interrogation.

"And now we've got a problem," Clark commented wryly after the prisoners had been questioned. "We can't release these Reds. They'd spread the word about us sure as thunder."

"Let's shoot 'em," Joe suggested realistically.

"No. Put 'em to work building a stockade, then

keep 'em inside. We can pick guard details from the Army."

In the course of the next week and a half *Flagship* bagged several more sampans. Altogether thirty-two boats of various sizes were captured. Some surrendered immediately. A few offered token resistance. Only Twantze attacked with an "armada" — to be badly beaten.

Each night, following the questioning of prisoners, Clark's wireless reports to Tokyo became longer. Then his youthful spies began returning from the mainland, and the reports became more detailed. The keen-eyed, alert boys were doing a fine job. They related their observations of enemy forces, guns, emplacements. They had even measured the height of the seawall in the Inchon tidal basin so that Clark could wireless Tokyo specifications for ladders to be carried in assault boats.

One by one the boys returned and checked in at headquarters. By the end of five days the last one came back safely, much to Clark's relief. Things are coming along fine, he told himself.

Then, on September 11, Commander Lee raised a question. He politely informed Rear Admiral Doyle that he doubted the accuracy of the United States

Navy tide tables for Inchon. It seemed probable to him that a series of typhoons had upset the old tables. This was serious. With the tremendous thirty-foot tides and swift current on the Inchon coast, any miscalculation of tide by an invasion fleet might well disrupt an assault time schedule and bring disaster. The planning board sent an imperative request to Clark to check the United States Navy time schedule.

On the night of September 11, shortly after Clark received Lee's message, young Sienso bobbed into the headquarters tent with alarming news. "Make-believe fishing at Taebu-do," he declared. "Twantze made like wasp. Now has many gun, many men. Bimeby tomorrow he come *boom-boom* island good."

"The devil you say," Clark muttered and stared at Sammy.

The interpreter nodded. Like that of all the other boys, Sienso's information was entirely to be trusted.

"There's been a lot of activity over at Taebu-do last few days, Lieutenant," Sammy agreed. "Twantze's getting ready to do something."

Clark thought rapidly. Here was this urgent job which Tokyo had asked him to do. It would take up his time on the following day. He couldn't afford to fight off an all-out attack. There was no other way —

he decided swiftly — he must have help. Whereupon he wirelessed Tokyo for what he hated most to ask — assistance.

He received it promptly. At dawn on the twelfth, the United States destroyer *Hanson* appeared off Yonghung-do with Commander Cecil R. Welte on the bridge. Welte didn't know what Clark was doing on the little island. But if he was curious, he didn't show it.

"What am I to do?" he asked. "Take you back to Sasebo?"

Clark shook his head. "No. That's Taebu-do over there. It's under command of Captain Twantze. I'd like to have the daylights clobbered out of it."

"A positive pleasure," Welte beamed.

Captain Twantze, thirsting for revenge, was loading men aboard his invasion fleet of sampans when the *Hanson* began dropping H.E. shells on the island. Five minutes later he scuttled for cover with his men.

Back in Tokyo the High Command decided to give Clark still further co-operation. Corsairs with rockets and 500-pound bombs came winging over Taebu-do. They blew the invasion sampans to pieces and gave the island a terrific shelling. And the entire village of

Yonghung-do, headed by the Young Men's Association, gathered on the shore to watch.

Clark made new tide observations and discovered that Commander Lee had been right. As a result of typhoons and recent oceanic disturbances the United States Navy's tide tables were in error by five all-important minutes. Clark wirelessed his information to Tokyo without the slightest interruption from Taebu-do.

The heavy bombardment of the island, however, did not pass unnoticed on Inchon and Wolmi-do. The Reds knew that something unusual was up. The entire coast was on the alert. The *Hanson* had been observed off Yonghung-do before sailing back to Sasebo.

They're bound to investigate our island before long to find out what's cooking, Clark thought to himself grimly. I've got to complete Mission X before they come.

Mission X was part of the top-secret assignment entrusted to Clark, one to be executed personally by him. On his judgment depended the life — or death — of thousands of men in the invasion to come. What the U. N. High Command wanted to know, and still did not know, was whether it was *practical* to land an assault force from the sea.

Late at night, Clark and four men — Sienso, Hayjun, Soji Iwon and Sammy — set out from the island aboard *Flagship*. Cautiously Soji Iwon steered for the ship channel, then headed towards Inchon under the moonless sky. Clark read his watch. It was 10:30 P.M. and the tide was running out fast. Two miles from Inchon he ordered Soji Iwon to cut the engine. Sienso and Hayjun put the small rubber boat over the side.

Clark entered it with Sammy, and at once began bucking the strong current towards Inchon. For half a mile they paddled hard. Then the blades of their paddles struck mud. A few yards further and their tiny craft was stopped by thick, slimy gumbo.

"Wait here," Clark ordered Sammy tautly. "If you hear a grenade, paddle back to *Flagship* without me."

Sammy nodded silently. He knew why Clark carried the grenade. The lieutenant would not be taken alive.

Clark removed his sneakers and placed them in the bottom of the tiny boat. He rolled up the pants legs of his fatigues and stepped out. His legs sank up to the knees in the soft gumbo. Slowly he started for the nearest Inchon beach almost a mile and a quarter away. The mud became firmer, scarcely reaching to his ankles.

He kept on moving. Suddenly he was floundering deep in the treacherous gumbo again. Up to his chest. Doggedly he fought his way forward, step by step until he reached the beach. Drawing a deep breath he turned around and started back again.

I've found out what I want, he thought grimly. This would be a deathtrap under fire.

Exhausted, covered with slimy gumbo, he climbed at length into the rubber boat and paddled back to *Flagship* with Sammy.

Clark had completed Mission X.

Back in his tent he raised Tokyo and wirelessed his findings: *Report . . . Inchon not suitable for landing either troops or vehicles across the mud.*

On D-day, the United States 10th Corps, First Marine Division and Seventh Division, made an amphibious landing on Wolmi-do, securing it in two hours. Some eleven hours later the First Marines and ROK marine battalions stormed Inchon.

There was but one area where tanks, trucks and other heavy equipment essential to success could possibly be put ashore at Inchon — on the waterfront, facing the city streets. The attacking U. N. forces knew right where to put it. They also knew a great many other things about Inchon, Wolmi-do, and Kimpo airfield, to the considerable surprise of the enemy.

The consternation of the defending Reds was a great satisfaction to Lieutenant Eugene Franklin Clark, United States Navy and Commander in Chief of the Young Men's Association of Yonghung-do. He had spent more than two weeks and lost forty pounds gathering this vital information right under their noses.

The General from the Pentagon

by Francis Chase, Jr.

THE DAY Grattan English took over Division — five days after General Hanley had lost his life in taking Hill 819 — there was a lull in the fighting. We still had possession of the hill, but the dispossessed Chinese had battled fiercely to retake it, until last night. It wasn't a restful lull. We — the general and I — had been in Korea only twenty-four hours, and at his new Division less than twelve hours; but we could sense the uneasy calm that had settled over the valley floor.

But it was a lull, nevertheless, and the general had taken advantage of it to climb the shell-tortured hill with Easy Company, of the 47th Infantry Regiment.

"Want to go along, Ding?" he asked me.

"Sure," I said, but I wondered if he ought to go. After all, he wasn't running a regiment now. He had

a couple of stars on his shoulders. Besides, it had been
a long time since he'd been in the field; seven years.
He sensed my feeling, I guess.

"Maps are all right," he said, "but they never take
the place of personal observation. There's always
something — a ditch, maybe a little rise where a machine gun should be sited — that might not show up
on a map but which could spell the difference between winning and getting your ears pinned back.
Especially in this sort of fighting." He didn't fool me
for a minute; that was only part of his reason for
wanting to climb that hill. He went on, "I figure we
can go up with Easy Company, which is to relieve
Fox Company atop the knob, have a quick look-see,
and then come back to our line with Fox Company."

It wasn't a bad climb that morning, with the early
sun shining in our faces. But in the burnt-out splotches
of the rice paddies, scorched by white sulphur shells,
and in the shallow holes where mortar fire, like a pox,
had scarred the hillside, it was easy to figure out how
it had been coming up this hill five nights before.
Near the top, Captain Fisher, of Easy Company, led
the way into a shallow trench. Then, in single file and
bent over so that our silhouettes were well below the
skyline, we followed the trench up onto the tabletop

of the hill. The captain of Fox Company was waiting for us.

The general's eyes twinkled. "Hello, Roger," he said. "It's been a long time."

"Why, Grat — General!" The captain was only a kid — the general's kid brother — and he didn't quite know what to say, seeing the stars on his brother's shoulders for the first time. With his men looking on curiously, he ended up by saluting stiffly. "I heard you were getting Division, but — well, I never expected to see you come through that trench. I don't know why —"

"Maybe," the general finished for him, "it's because you keep thinking of me behind a desk in the Pentagon, or pouring cocktails on the veranda at Georgetown."

The kid's face went crimson. Maybe he had been thinking what the general thought. After all, Roger was too young for the war and the way he remembered his brother — in those years when he was still at the Point — was behind a Pentagon desk or at cocktail parties. But maybe it was like Ellen — Ellen's the general's wife — said. Maybe Grat was getting a complex about those stars. He knew what people back in Washington were saying — that his father-in-law,

Senator Leger, had more to do with the stars Grattan English wore on his shoulders than Grattan English did.

They were wrong, of course. If you'd been with Grat in Hürtgen Forest or at Jülich, you'd have known they were wrong. But it hadn't done him any good to know what they were saying. I'd been sort of glad they'd finally given him a combat command, especially when he name-requested me to go along as his G-3. I figured it was just what he needed, to show, once and for all, that he had the stuff it took; a chance for him to get rid of the doubts that were beginning to eat at his insides.

All the way out on the plane, he'd been like a kid flying to the North Pole to meet Santa Claus. Then, last night, that briefing at Corps, and he was right back where he started from. Even I could figure out that this wasn't so much a briefing as it was a kind of appraising process. Oh, they'd gone through all the motions. General Desmond, the Corps commander, had gone to the war tent with us, introduced us to the officers we didn't know. Then the G-staff went into action — problems of terrain, replacements, logistics, enemy potentialities.

But it was really a lot of one-star generals and bird

colonels, with years and experience far beyond his, trying to figure out just what Grattan English had on the ball. They knew what he'd done in Europe, all right, but it didn't take a mind reader to know what they were thinking. In Europe, he'd had a regiment — not a division. And it was a different sort of war from this. You could almost hear them wondering — politely, and maybe a little enviously — if, after all, the best way to get ahead in this man's Army wasn't to marry the daughter of an influential member of the Senate Armed Forces Committee. In the Air Force, a major general at forty-two might be routine, but not in the infantry. At any rate, I could see it wasn't going to be a bed of roses, this command, with a couple of dozen pairs of eyes watching for any little slip-up, and a lot of guys figuring they knew more about the kind of fighting that went on in these hills than Grat.

The moment the general had snapped at the kid, I could see he was sorry. His face went red and there was a kind of shock in his eyes, seeing the old-young face of his brother. Fatigue had etched deep lines under the blue stubble of the captain's beard, and there were cavernous hollows under his eyes. A couple of weeks of rest and recuperation would do something about the fatigue lines. But they wouldn't erase what had come to rest in his eyes — the dark shadows of Seoul and the Pusan Perimeter, the bloody battle for Hill 819.

"I'm going back to Division with your company, Roger," the general said. "But first, I'd like to take a quick look around."

We started walking, Grat taking in the layout of the trenches, the siting of the mortar section, the machine-gun emplacements. But there was something else that I noticed: the growing hostility in the men of Fox Company. Their relief was here, the enemy was quiet. They wanted to get back to Division line before anything happened, and they'd been out here long enough to have a rough idea of some of the things that could happen.

Then, suddenly, young English was telling about the night General Hanley died and the fight for the hilltop. It was as if, once started, he had to get it all out of his system. The general let him talk it out, even though he could take one look about him and figure it out for himself. The hill was scorched of the sparse vegetation that had once covered it, and it still had that sour powder-and-death smell. A network of trenches and dugouts, with the dirt that had been thrown out of them, gave the knob a fresh, red-brown ugliness. Below us, on the north, were the few charred frames of a village, Tongwon-ni, which had once nestled in what its founders mistakenly considered the protection of the hillside.

Captain Fisher hurried up.

"Excuse me, sir, but enemy patrols are moving in behind us."

That old feeling of excitement and unease raced again through my blood, and I was glad that, like before, the excitement outweighed the unease. We strode through the trenches to the opposite side of the hilltop, bellied up the side of a trench, and played our field glasses across the battered slope we'd just finished climbing. I could feel the short hairs on my neck go stiff as I caught a fleeting glimpse of a figure scurrying from one shellhole to another. Moments later, a second figure followed the first. After that, at different points on the slope, I could see similar movements.

"We could 'a' been back in the line by now," a sergeant of Fox Company grumbled to his squad, waiting near the shallow trench which, moments before, had seemed the doorway to safety. His voice went sarcastic. "But, no — the general has to go sight-seeing!"

The sergeant's voice had been low, but in the tense quiet I had no trouble hearing his words. Captain Fisher and young English heard them, too, but they pretended they didn't. So did Grattan English. Maybe he didn't mind the griping; the best soldiers were gripers. But I had an idea he was remembering, from back in Germany, that although he had been much younger then, his men never spoke of him among themselves as the colonel. He had always been the Old Man. But then, Grattan knew, too, that the kind of affection and respect a soldier put into that term didn't come quickly. A man had to earn it.

"I could lay some mortar fire down there, sir," Fisher said, "or we could call for Division artillery."

The two captains — English and Fisher — were eying the general curiously. They were deferring to his judgment. But I had a feeling it was a deference born of curiosity more than respect for that judgment. This was the sort of thing they had dealt with for two years; knowing how to deal with it was the difference between living and dying. Now they were curious to see how a general, who had spent that two years in the Pentagon, would handle himself, threatened with infiltration and cut off from the safety of Division.

I think the general felt it, just as I did. And it was a

sort of weird feeling — watching this kid brother that Grat had nursed through his teens, and who'd have to live a hundred years to grow up into half the man Grat was, putting the screws on now.

The general took it in his stride.

"We'll wait and see what they're up to," he said calmly. "If it's just a patrol action, Fox Company can take care of it on the way down. If it's something more — well, we'll wait and see."

He swung his glasses back onto the slope. But I didn't miss the looks Fisher and the kid exchanged, nor their meaning — portrait of a two-star general making a mountain out of a molehill.

With anyone else, I'd have been inclined to agree with the two company commanders. The thing to do was sprinkle a lot of mortar fire over the slope, then move down and clean it out. But when you'd gone through three years of fighting under Grattan English, first in North Africa and then from Normandy to Magdeburg, you knew a lot better. He had a sort of sixth sense about enemy intentions, a quick way of sizing up a situation and deciding what to do about it. It wasn't command by hunch. It was the end product of training, know-how, tactical appreciation and exercise of judgment.

"That's more than just a patrol or two cutting behind us, Ding," he said to me. "Figure the thing out. Hill 819 commands this whole valley — it's valuable real estate. The enemy's been trying to bull his way back up the hill without any luck, so now he's resorting to tricks."

"That could be, Grat," I said. I lowered my voice. "I'm afraid, though, that our junior GHQ here is inclined to disagree."

The general didn't crack a smile. His mind seemed to be far away.

"Do you remember last night, back at Corps, when we were talking to Colonel Hawthorne? He said he used to play chess with Cheng-fu in Peking —"

"Sure," I replied. "I remember exactly what he said. He said, 'Before the war, when I was military attaché at Peking, I used to know the general who commands the Chinese corps opposite your division — Cheng-fu. He used to teach math at the university there, and twice a week we used to play chess. The best I ever ran into, that fellow — cunning, ruthless, completely unorthodox. When the Japs marched into Manchuria,

he joined up with Chiang. Became one of his best officers. In 1946, he defected to the Commies.' That's
what he said, Grat, but you know — the way he kept
squinting at you across the table, like an old man giving a boy good advice he was sure the boy wouldn't
bother to take — I had a feeling maybe he was trying
to say a lot more than just that."

"I think you're right, Ding. I think he did say a lot
more than what he seemed to say."

The men of Fox Company were becoming particularly unhappy. Even Captain English began to look
anxiously at his brother as the sun climbed in the
heaven. But anxiety wasn't all that was in Roger English's eyes. There was a shame there, too — at his
brother's indecision in the presence of a minor enemy
force that any second john, fresh out of Riley, would
know how to handle without thinking.

"Don't you think, sir, we ought to be starting down
— before they throw too much strength between us
and Division?"

It wasn't really a question; it was a suggestion. As if,
after all, *someone* in the English family had to take the
bull by the horns.

"I think that's exactly what they want us to do, Roger."

Again I caught the quick look, flashed from one captain to the other. I could have batted their heads together, but the general, with his sweet disposition, passed it over.

"I think it's a trap — a small trap which is part of a bigger trap," he went on. I knew how he must feel — like a guinea pig in a medical laboratory. On one side, the professors at Corps were watching him critically. After all, Grat was new to this kind of war, whereas they were old hands at it. From the other side, the company-level students — including his own kid brother — were just as critical. There wasn't much he could do about Corps, but if I'd had Grat's stars for ten minutes I'd have put the kids in their place.

"Well, what are we going to do, sir? Wait for them to spring their trap?"

Indictment and insolence were in Captain English's question. For the first time in years, I saw the spark of anger highlight the general's eyes, the round little red spots come out on his cheeks.

"Something like that, Captain," he said sharply. "But all you'll have to concern yourself with is obeying my orders. Nothing very much is going to happen till after dark, but we'll be ready just in case. Easy Company will defend the south slope, Fox Company the north. Dispose your men at once. In event of an attack, each company is responsible for defending its own share of the perimeter. Unless I issue orders to the contrary, no one will leave his post to help anyone else. Is that clear, gentlemen?"

The captains eyed each other again, but quickly this time. "Yes, sir," they said in unison, saluting and moving off to carry out the general's orders.

We were all alone in the little piece of connecting trench. The general just stood there, kicking the dirt with the toe of his boot.

"Tell me something, Grat," I said. "When we were that age, did we know as much as the kids think they know today?"

The general grinned sort of sheepishly.

"I shouldn't have flown off like that," he said. "I'm sure we thought we knew a lot more. You know, Ding — for seven years I've been cursing a desk assignment. Grat, I'd say to myself every hour on the hour, this isn't for you. You're a field soldier. I figure a guy with two stars on his shoulder should have a division. Then, just today, I learn something: I learn how much I really learned in those seven years in Operations and Plans."

He lit a cigarette and took a deep drag.

"Seven years ago — and I was already a bird colonel then — I'd have been thinking about this operation the way those kids do — as a small-unit action to be snuffed out quickly by a one-company attack down the slope and a limited attack from Division. Now, when I look at a small-unit tactic, I find myself trying to fit it into the broader pattern of which it's part. When you have a company, you think on company level. When you get a division, you have to spread yourself a bit. The Army expects a lot more from a man with two stars than it does from a man with two bars, Ding."

My oak leaf lifted me out of the two-bar class, but I still didn't belong in the higher galaxy. I didn't have the slightest idea what the general had figured out. I said as much.

"Let's put it this way," he said. "Cheng-fu is a guy who'll lose his pawns without tears so long as they buy him something. Those fellows out there" — he waved at the south slope where the Chinese had infiltrated — "are pawns. Cheng's given us this alternative: to move in and wipe them out, or to watch and wait, leaving them alone till they make a move. Suppose we choose the first course and move in to wipe them out. One thing is sure — Cheng's got every piece of artillery he owns zeroed-in, on that slope, and the moment we're out there in force he lowers the boom."

"But his own men are out there too," I objected.

"But they're only pawns. Remember that Cheng's a chess player. Any day Cheng can lose two or three hundred Chinese to kill the same number of Americans, he's had a good day. A couple of years like that, he wins the war."

"Okay," I said. "So we watch and wait. Then what happens?"

"Then maybe we'll fall into another Cheng trap — a bigger one. When dark comes, he launches an attack up the south slope with his pawns. We rush to the south side of the hill, to defend it, and — bingo! Cheng's knights — his *real* force — attack up the north slope, overrun us, and the Chinks have bought themselves a hill."

I wasn't so sure from anything Grat had said so far but that maybe Fisher and young English were right — wipe out the pawns while we still had time, so we could defend ourselves against the knights.

"You think, with two companies, we can hold this hill against a frontal and rear attack in force, General?"

"Only for a while," he said. "But long enough for our purposes." He took a map from his pocket and spread it out on the floor of the trench. "What we're going to do, Ding, is let Cheng play chess while we play baseball — a kind of squeeze play."

He located Hill 819 on the map. It stood up, like a sore thumb, from the valley floor. Some four miles to the south — at the first defensible point, a creek bed in the valley floor — was our division line. The enemy line was about the same distance away, toward the north, where the foothills started to rise. The hill was in a sort of no man's land, with a good six miles of flat valley floor stretching away on either side, east and west, to the side walls of the valley.

"When it's dark, Cheng won't be the only one to start moving men," the general said. "I'm going to order the 73rd Regiment to be ready to move, after dark, to this point" — he laid a long finger on the map, two miles north of Hill 819 and far off to the west — "and the 87th will move at the same time to this point." His finger fell on a point opposite the other, two miles north of the hill but on the east.

I could begin to see what he had in mind now. The

two regiments, moving quietly under darkness in wide, flanking movements, were like a couple of football ends sneaking around the enemy's backs to receive a pass.

"Two companies here on the hill should be able to give a pretty good account of themselves," he went on, "until Cheng has committed his main force. Then I fire a flare up here, and the 73rd and the 87th attack Cheng's flanks — a pincers movement. With real surprise, we might land quite a bag."

The general had set up his CP in the radio dugout. Now came the part of battle he hated most — the waiting. I used to watch him chew his nails in the Hürtgen Forest, waiting for the hour of attack. He was biting them now — and smoking one cigarette after another.

Everything that Grattan could do had been done. Battalion had been instructed, by runner, and had sent orders back committing Easy Company and suspending relief of Fox indefinitely. Then, over the radio, with scrambler attached, Grat had given his orders to General Willett, the assistant division commander, back at division headquarters. The moment it was dark, Willett was to set the two regiments in motion, holding the 47th in reserve. General Willett had been a little doubtful about the whole thing.

"I can't sit here and argue over radio," Grattan had snapped. "Just see that the regiments are closed on their LD's when the flare signal goes up and that they know what they're to do. If Cheng doesn't attack no harm's done."

That was where Grat was wrong. If — after he'd set two regiments in motion, pulling them out of the line — the Chinese didn't attack, he could be laughed out of the Army. It wasn't as if he'd been out here for months. He was new to the Far East Command, he was young, and there were plenty of people in Korea who felt they had a better title to his command. I could almost see the old heads at Corps wag knowingly at word that the young general — such a whiz at the Pentagon and in the formal combat of Europe, in World War II — had been cut off from his division the first morning he had it.

And that was where they were wrong. Grattan English's stars were no gift from any man. He'd earned them, on plenty of battlefields where his regimental combat team had earned the Germans' accolade, "Roosevelt's SS Troop." He'd earned them in Washington, where his appreciation of the Yalu disaster showed him to be a prime fighting man who knew when to stay in there swinging and when it was best to pull back and fight another day. Most of the Plans and Ops people were thinking in terms of evacuation when the Chinese struck at the Yalu. Not Grat. His study of the situation turned the tide of thinking — to sticking on and winning back what we'd lost.

When you're waiting like this, time moves — but slowly, like a snail inching his way along a slimy rock. Dark came suddenly, the way it comes out here, like a blanket being plopped over your head quickly, from behind. I lit a candle, sticking it to the top of an old rations box with its wax drippings.

The general stretched out on the radioman's bunk, but he didn't close his eyes.

"Just about now," he said, "Ellen's sitting down to dinner, I guess. I tried to get her to move in with her father while I was away, but she wouldn't. She said, 'This is our home, Grat — filled with our things and our memories.' "

He took a deep drag on his cigarette. We'd been together a long time — ever since Benning — and when you go through the things we'd gone through together, you know what the other guy's thinking before he opens his mouth. Just as I knew what he was thinking about now. I even knew what had reminded him of it — the candle.

He was thinking about that last night, before we left for Korea. We'd got the word about four o'clock one afternoon that we'd be catching the plane at eight the next morning. The general asked me to come home to dinner with him and Ellen. Ordinarily, a fellow'd want that last evening alone — especially when the girl was Ellen. Grat wanted that, too, but, even more, he wanted moral support. Ellen wasn't like so many Army wives who'd been Army brats before becoming Army wives. She didn't give a hoot for the stars; what she loved was Grat. She could never understand why he itched for a combat command. Maybe she thought that the way Grat kept worrying the department for a Korean assignment, she'd failed him in some way.

She was upstairs that night when we came in. He mixed me a Martini and went upstairs. They were up there a long time. When they finally came down and dinner was served, we ate by candlelight.

"Can't we have a little light, dear?" he had protested. "I can't see what I'm eating. More important"

— he laughed, but there was a lot of truth in what he said — "I can't see you."

Ellen laughed too — a mellow, tinkling little laugh that went with her fragile beauty; a musical sort of laugh, but with sad music. But we ate by candlelight. I always thought she didn't want me — or Grat, either — to see the places where tears had streaked her cheeks.

It was an odd thing that she should feel that, in some way, she had failed him. That was the way Grat had felt too. He'd laid a lot on the line tonight — maybe whether he could ever go back and feel at ease with Ellen again although, more than anything else, I knew that was what he wanted.

2300 hours. The general checked his flare gun for the tenth time, opened a fresh pack of cigarettes. There was no sign of enemy action. The C rations I'd eaten lay heavy in my stomach. So did my guilt. I felt guilty questioning his judgment. Everybody else did — even the kid brother who had once idolized him and in whom Grat thought the sun rose and set. Now I was beginning to feel it too. Maybe it would have been better to have taken care of that infiltrating party. That was all anyone expected. After all, this was a different kind of war from Europe — this was a small-unit war.

The general stood up and walked to the door of the dugout. I wondered if, in the thick boiled-coffee-and-sweat smell of the place, he sensed my doubts. I also wondered why any man in his right mind would choose this way to make a living.

"Think I'll take one more look around," he said, stepping outside. I joined him. The night was dark and quiet; almost too quiet. A night bird whistled mournfully, off in the distance. I wondered if it was really a bird. "You know, Ding — it'd be funny if the kids were right."

But I knew that it wouldn't be funny for Grat. He had one chance — only one — of ever winning back the respect of his kid brother. He'd laid that on the line tonight too.

That was when the first wave attacked up the south slope, yelling and screaming like banshees. I could feel the goose pimples run up and down my spine. Captain English came trotting through the connecting trench.

"They're hitting us hard from the south, sir. Shouldn't I send a couple of platoons over to help Easy Company, sir?"

I'm sure that all the same doubts that had been gnawing away at my insides had been gnawing away at Grat's too. But now you could see the old instincts and reactions grow sharp, self-confidence come flowing back.

"You have your orders, Captain," he said sharply. "See that you obey them." In the dim light that flickered out through the dugout door, you could see the hurt look in the kid's eyes at the peremptory tone. "You'll have all you can do on that side, soon, Roger," the general added, a bit softer.

And he was right, the way he always seemed to be right in estimating an enemy's capabilities. That was when the first wave hit the north side of the hill. Only, on the north side, the waves were so close together that the charging walls of human flesh seemed to be almost solid.

"He must have five thousand men down there," Grat said. It was one of the few moments he was still. For the first twenty minutes of the attack, he was everywhere. Once, I'd dragged him back out of a first-line trench on the north slope where he'd been tossing hand grenades.

"They're getting in!"

The shout — loud above the sound of battle —

came from the north side of the hill. Grat started off on the run in that direction.

A handful of men were fighting a hand-to-hand fight with Chinese who had overrun the trench. Waiting was hard for the general, but this he loved. Clubbing his forty-five, he leaped into the trench.

I knew there was no use trying to get him out. From just above, I heard the dull crunch of his gun butt against a Chinese head. And just in time, too, for the Chinese was about to bring a murderous blade down into the unprotected back of a sergeant, struggling with another Chinese.

For a brief second, the sergeant turned and, seeing the general standing above the unconscious Chinese, grinned. It was the sergeant who had grumbled that morning about the general's sight-seeing.

Then, convinced that Cheng had committed his full force, the general lifted his flare-gun and fired. As the red flare arched slowly in the dark heaven, you could see the Chinese below — so close that their elbows were rubbing. But it was another half hour of nip-and-tuck atop the hill before the pressure began to let up — before Cheng's troops realized that a trap had been sprung, and that it wasn't theirs.

It was dawn before we were able to count our bag, even roughly — some two thousand Chinese dead, more than five thousand captured. The flank attacks had achieved complete surprise, rolling through the unsuspecting mass of Cheng's attackers like a hot knife searing through butter.

A corporal came to tell the general he was wanted in the radio dugout. General Desmond from Corps was at the other end.

"Just got the news, Grat," the corps commander said jubilantly. "Most decisive thing's happened out here in months. Like Colonel Hawthorne just said — a little imagination goes a long way. But listen, Grat — you keep out of those forward posts after this. You and I — we're getting too old for that kind of thing."

The general tried to answer, but he felt his voice choke up.

"Thank you, sir," he managed to say finally. "And thank Colonel Hawthorne too. It was mostly his imagination that's responsible."

He handed the receiver back to the radioman and walked to the door. In the cold gray light, his brother was waiting.

"Grat — Captain Fisher and I want to say . . ." He halted, searching again for words that the sheepish expression on his face made unnecessary. "Well, we're both . . ."

From around a bend in the trench, out of sight, a high, whining sort of voice carried through the quiet.

"You think maybe now we get relieved, Sarge?"

"It's a cinch," the sergeant answered.

The general might live to be a hundred, but he'd never forget that voice which, yesterday morning, was sarcastically blaming him for putting the men of Fox Company in such a spot. But this time, none of us made any pretense; we all listened — the general, Roger and I.

"It's a dead-pan cinch," the sergeant repeated himself. "The Old Man'll see to that!"

The general turned away, as if to study a long column of Chinese prisoners moving southward across the valley floor. Roger and I moved off too. After all, the sergeant had said all that there was to say.

The Chaplain of Company C

by William Chamberlain

CHARLEY COMPANY — what was left of it — came down out of the hills in the July afternoon. There was a town down here among the rice paddies. Not much of a town — maybe thirty-odd straw-thatched houses squatting in the rain. In a few of them people peered from the doors — brown-faced, white-clad people. Most of the people, though, had already fled southward before the North Korean tanks which were coming up the valley from Taejon.

Lieutenant Norton sat in one of the two jeeps which were all that Charley Company had left now. His face was muddy and drawn and tired, and he wore a dirty bandage around his left arm. He was the only officer left with Charley Company. The only officer, that is, except Captain Joyce, and Captain Joyce didn't count. He was a chaplain. A noncombatant who didn't belong up here in the first place. That was the way that Sergeant Kruger felt about it. Captain Joyce had just joined them that morning, a little while before Charley Company had been chased out of its last delaying position.

Now Sergeant Kruger came through the mud of the narrow street to lean an arm on the jeep's side. He was a heavy, graying man who had grown old in wars, and he didn't like the way things were going. He had just finished making the rounds and checking up on things, and he didn't like it at all. Lieutenant Norton could feel the sergeant's uneasiness as he sat there in the rain.

"Well?" he asked sharply.

Lieutenant Norton didn't mean to speak so sharply, but he was very young, and too many hours without sleep had bitten into him too deeply. Then, too, there was that gnawing pain in his side which he hadn't mentioned to anyone yet. It wasn't bleeding much, and he hoped that everything was going to be all right. Deep down within him, though, he knew that it wasn't.

"Forty-nine left, countin' the padre," Sergeant Kruger told him. "Eleven of 'em wounded . . . not too bad."

"What's this about a padre?" Lieutenant Norton asked tiredly. He didn't really care much.

Sergeant Kruger shrugged his shoulders. "He got lost from one of the other regiments, I guess. I never seen him before."

Lieutenant Norton nodded — a slow nod like that of an old man dozing in a chair in front of a fire. "We'll rest here a little. Then we'll go south and look for the rest of the outfit." He stopped for a minute, and then added soberly, "If the gooks let us."

He didn't know exactly where they would go. He didn't know exactly what they would do, either. It was thirty hours now since Charley Company had had any contact with the battalion. He guessed, though, that if they kept on going south they'd eventually run into Americans somewhere.

"Yes, sir," Sergeant Kruger said. He voiced the worry that had been gnawing at him. "You got any idea where we are or where the rest of the outfit is, Lieutenant?"

"Have you?" Lieutenant Norton asked sharply again. Pain had suddenly grabbed at his side and the straw-thatched houses in front of him were starting to shimmer fantastically in the rain.

Sergeant Kruger shook his head. "I guess I been

runnin' too fast to keep track," he said. "You better come over and lay down out of the rain for a little bit, Lieutenant. You don't look so good."

Lieutenant Norton tried to say that he was all right, but the words wouldn't come and the houses were dancing up and down more violently now. He put his head down against the jeep's wheel to make the pictures stop dancing.

From a great distance he could hear Sergeant Kruger calling, "Kalinsky! Come give me a hand with the lieutenant! He's been hit again!"

The little thread of worry became deeper and more solid in Sergeant Kruger as they carried Lieutenant Norton into the shelter of one of the houses and laid him on the floor. Kalinsky, the medical-aid man, knelt and opened the front of the lieutenant's rain-soaked shirt. Other men crowded at the door, faces uneasy. Lieutenant Norton was a good officer. They liked him and now it looked as though he had had it . . . the same as Captain Fanning and the others had had it.

"He's took it bad, Sarge," Kalinsky said morosely, prodding with gentle fingers. "The gooks must of got him when we pulled off that last hill."

It was bad, all right, Sergeant Kruger knew. You

didn't have to look twice at the lieutenant to see that he wasn't going to do any more fighting for a long time. Maybe never. Kalinsky plugged the hole, working expertly with his big fingers, while Sergeant Kruger sat on his heels and watched. The faces at the doorway irritated him vaguely. They kept reminding him that he was on his own now, and he didn't like that. He was the senior noncom left, and the responsibility of command was already beginning to worry him.

"O'Daniel," he said sharply to one of the faces at the door, "take a detail and outpost the road. The rest of you get some rest."

The men went away and Sergeant Kruger rubbed his hands on his muddy trousers and felt for a cigarette. Then he remembered that he had run out of cigarettes yesterday, and that bothered him too. Kalinsky tied the bandage and stood up.

"Best I can do," he said. "He ought to be evacuated."

"Well, we can't evacuate him or anybody else until we got some place to evacuate 'em to," Sergeant Kruger said roughly. "Stay with him."

"Okay," Kalinsky said. He glanced a little doubtfully at Kruger.

The latter could feel Kalinsky's uncertainty, and it increased his own irritation and pushed that worry up into the front of his mind again. He felt that somehow a dirty trick had been played on him. He was just a sergeant. He wasn't supposed to command a company. The book said that, and all of his life he had gone by the book.

A man came through the doorway, cutting off the light of the fading afternoon for a moment, and Kruger saw that it was the chaplain. A lean, rangy man in his thirties, dressed in battle clothes and with no insignia — either of rank or of the church — visible on him. Sergeant Kruger had never seen him before this morning. All he knew was that his name was Joyce and that he was a captain chaplain.

Captain Joyce looked at the lieutenant and said, "Bad, Sergeant?" and Sergeant Kruger nodded, a little resentfully. He had always observed a strict neutrality toward chaplains. He didn't dislike them exactly, he just wanted them to stay on their own side of the street while he stayed on his.

"Pretty bad," he said.

"Let me have a look."

Joyce squatted on his heels above the lieutenant and put fingers to his wrist; then probed a little at the lieutenant's side without disturbing the bandage. He didn't like what he found. Lieutenant Norton mumbled and rolled his head and called for water.

Joyce said, "Give me your canteen, Sergeant."

"The book says you don't give 'em water when they got belly wounds," Kruger said.

Captain Joyce took the canteen and placed it on the floor while he eased Lieutenant Norton into a more comfortable position. Then he said gently, "There are times when the book could be wrong, Sergeant."

He tipped a thimbleful of water into the lieutenant's mouth, and Norton's tongue licked greedily at his cracked lips. "More," he said hoarsely.

"Not now. After a little while, Lieutenant," Joyce said. "Just take it easy. You'll be all right."

Norton laughed faintly. "Sure," he said. "Sure. I'll be all right." His eyes were too bright, Sergeant Kruger thought, and his face too flushed under the fuzz of blond beard. "You're the guy that joined up with us this morning, aren't you?" Norton went on.

"That's right," Joyce told him. "Just take it easy."

"You an officer? Somebody said you were an officer."

"Of sorts," Joyce said.

That deepened Sergeant Kruger's feeling of depression, and he went across to look out into the rain. He wondered if O'Daniel had set up an outpost . . . he had told him to. Nothing but kids in the Army these days, and you never knew for sure what they'd do. Not like the old Army. Maybe he ought to go check on O'Daniel. It would be bad to have the gook tanks come pouring into the town without any warning. Uncertainty held him, though, and after a minute he turned back into the room again.

"This outfit can use some officers," Lieutenant Norton was mumbling petulantly to Joyce. "What's your rank? You a lieutenant? You look awful old to be a lieutenant."

"A captain," Joyce said. "Now take it easy."

"You look awful old to be a captain, too," Norton said in a vague voice. "Well, I guess you better take over Charley Company until I get to feeling better. Don't feel very good."

"Rest awhile," Joyce said. "Everything will be all right."

Lieutenant Norton nodded at that. "Sure," he said again. "Sure. Just have a little nap. Haven't been sleeping so good lately. You take care of things . . . What'd you say your name was?"

"Joyce."

"Okay. You take care of things. Got to get a little nap."

He closed his eyes and Joyce watched him for a minute longer and then walked to the door, Sergeant Kruger following him. The rain was coming down in a steady drizzle. Joyce looked out, resting a hand on the door jamb, and Kruger waited.

For a moment Joyce's mind went back across the gap which almost ten years had made. There had been rice paddies then, too, and rain and the constant running back until his company — what was left of it — had come into the final standing ground at Bataan. He had worn the crossed rifles of the infantry on his collar in those days and he had not been much older than Lieutenant Norton. Later there had been the prison camps of Bilibid and Cabanatuan. And now the cycle had closed upon itself and there were rice paddies and rain and running again.

He shrugged the thoughts away. "You're the senior noncom?"

"Yes, sir," Sergeant Kruger answered.

"Good. I'm taking command until the lieutenant gets on his feet again," Joyce said. He didn't miss the look of shocked surprise in Kruger's face, and he knew the reason for it.

"Yes, sir," Kruger said again. "Does the cap'n mean —"

He stopped, letting his voice trail away. He had been expecting something like this but, now that it had happened, it seemed to be all wrong again. It was contrary to everything that he had been taught to believe during the thirty years that he had taken the Army's pay. A chaplain was a noncombatant. He didn't command troops. The book was explicit on that, and Sergeant Kruger believed in the book.

Joyce saw the indecision in Kruger's face and he smiled a little. "You don't like the idea, Sergeant?"

"It ain't exactly that, sir," Kruger said. "It's just —"

His voice died out again because he didn't know for sure what it was "just." Again he wished that he had a cigarette. He'd just concentrate on that, he thought, he wouldn't worry about the fact that a chaplain was commanding Charley Company. Then a new idea entered his head and he was aware of an almost exhilarating feeling of relief. He had just realized that if Captain Joyce took over Sergeant Kruger didn't have the responsibility any longer.

And it didn't really violate the book if you looked

at it in a sensible way. Lieutenant Norton was still commander of Charley Company until he was evacuated, and they couldn't evacuate him now because there was no place to evacuate him to. When they joined up with the battalion the colonel would certainly send some other officer to command the company. Actually, the padre was just acting for the lieutenant — sort of a deputy. That really made the thing right and legal.

The feeling of relief grew in Sergeant Kruger.

"Any orders, sir?" he asked. He'd help the captain all he could; he could do that fine.

Joyce wasn't listening. His mind was automatically checking over the things that had to be done. Funny, he thought, how quickly a man could drop back into the old habits of command.

When he spoke his voice was crisp and certain, "Have you got an outpost watching down the road?"

"Yes, sir. I told Corporal O'Daniel to go down there."

"How many men with him?"

Sergeant Kruger felt a little uncomfortable at the question. He didn't know the answer. Ordinarily he would have told O'Daniel how many men to take because he was usually meticulous with such details.

The collapse of Lieutenant Norton had upset him and he had forgotten.

"I don't know, sir," he said. "I was just going up there to check up on things."

"Never mind. I'll go," Joyce said. "I've got something else for you to do. Get what men we've got left organized into squads. I want to see the noncoms when I get back. Find out what weapons we've left and how the ammunition stands."

Sergeant Kruger said "Yes sir" smartly. He was feeling better now. Captain Joyce was saying things that made sense. "I'll have that done when the cap'n gets back."

Joyce nodded and went on out into the rain. At the jeep he paused and picked up the carbine which lay on the seat. It was muddy and he stopped long enough to wipe the action clean and test it. He'd have to make a point of that, he thought. Most of the men in Charley Company had never been in battle before and they hadn't learned yet that in battle a man lived or died according to the cleanliness of his weapon.

He followed the street through the town, and after a little the straw-thatched houses were behind him and he was on a road running between stone fences and bordered with trees. Rice paddies stretched on either side. It was an old road and in bad repair, and Joyce guessed that they were well off the main highway which led south from Taejon. That was good, in a way. Less likelihood of tanks jumping them.

The rain came down harder as he pushed on, alert for some sign of Corporal O'Daniel. Habit, coming swiftly back after ten years, caused him to move along the road's shoulder with his carbine ready. Soldiering was a little like learning to play the violin, he thought. Once learned, you never entirely forgot it.

Corporal O'Daniel and his two men had taken shelter in a culvert where a stream crossed the road some three hundred yards from the deserted town. At least it was partly dry under the culvert. At intervals one of the three would scramble the few feet up the bank, take a look along the stretch of road which ran straight ahead for a mile or more. Corporal O'Daniel was twenty-one and he had been in the Army just over two years.

"Nothing to see," he grunted as he slid down to the shelter of the culvert after having taken his look. "Road's as bare as the palm of your hand. No refugees even."

Littauer, a scarred man who had been a private in

the Army when O'Daniel had been playing with toys — and who was still a private — worried a chunk of tobacco off with his teeth; offered the plug to O'Daniel and Rube Henderson; put it back in his pocket when they refused.

"It can stay empty an' suit me fine," he said. "I ain't the warmongerin' kind. I've seen enough gooks already to last me if I live to be a hundred."

"What you giving us, pop?" O'Daniel said. "You're past a hundred now. I saw your service record. You were drawing pay back at the Battle of Bull Run."

"I been around," Littauer admitted complacently. "I've done my share of fightin' too."

"Sure you have," O'Daniel said. "I'll bet you're a holy terror in a brawl."

Littauer spat at the muddy water which flowed under the culvert. "I been in plenty of 'em," he said. "That wasn't the kind of fightin' I meant, though. Maybe you don't know it, but me an' General MacArthur liberated the Philippines singlehanded."

"Well, go on out there and liberate Korea then," O'Daniel said. "After you've got it liberated, I'll give it to you as a present. I don't want it."

"Shucks, I ain't in no hurry. Besides, I always got to have General MacArthur with me when I go liberatin'. We're a team. You know that skinny guy that joined up with us this morning?"

"I seen him. So what?"

"He's a chaplain," Littauer said. "Now what you suppose a chaplain is doin' up here?"

"Marrying people," O'Daniel said. "What do you think chaplains do? You want to get married?"

"Not me, kid. I was married once. It was worse than bein' in jail."

Rube Henderson sat a little apart from the others. He was twenty-seven and serious and a pretty good BAR man. He had a wife and a kid back in Shreveport, Louisiana, U.S.A., and he used to write to them every night before he had come here.

"You shouldn't talk that way about marriage," he said to Littauer. "Marriage is the most sacred thing there is."

Littauer blinked and spat again at the muddy water. "Maybe my old woman didn't know about that. The last time I saw her she wanted to cut me up with a butcher knife."

"Just the same, it's sacred," Rube Henderson insisted doggedly. "You shouldn't talk about it that way."

"Okay. Okay. It's sacred," Littauer said. "She still

wanted to cut me up. Take a look at the road. It's your turn."

Henderson was starting to climb the bank when Joyce slid down, his feet sinking deeply into the mud at the stream's edge. Corporal O'Daniel sat still and looked at him, but Littauer saw something in Joyce's face that brought him to his feet.

"Which one of you is Corporal O'Daniel?" Joyce asked.

"That's me, chum," O'Daniel said.

"You're supposed to be outposting this road, Corporal?" Joyce asked gently.

"Sure, Padre. That's the general idea if you're —"

"And if I had been a North Korean, you'd all be dead right now. Isn't that right?"

O'Daniel realized that this picture was out of focus somehow, and struggled sheepishly to his feet. Joyce's eyes took a deeper spark and there was a quality in his voice that brought Littauer to a stiff attention.

"And the rest of the company, back in town, would probably be dead too," Joyce went on. "There are a lot of things I can overlook, O'Daniel. That's not one of them. You're Private O'Daniel now." He swung around to Littauer. "You're an old soldier?"

"Yes, sir."

"Good. I'm Captain Joyce, commanding Charley Company right now. Where'd you serve in the last war?"

"New Guinea, sir. Philippines."

"You won't find anything different here. You're acting corporal from now on. What's your name?"

"Littauer, sir."

A flash of humor softened Joyce's mouth. "Twenty years in the Army and ten of them in the guardhouse, I'll bet. That right?"

Littauer grinned and relaxed. "The cap'n must of been readin' my service record," he said. "I've had the stripes put on me an' took off again so many times that I've lost count."

"Okay, bring your detail and follow me, Littauer."

The four of them scrambled up the bank and went along the road for fifty yards to where a section of the rock fence had spilled out into a waist-high heap. There was brush here and the line of trees provided a covered route back to the town.

"Put your BAR man here," Joyce said curtly. "You can cover the bottleneck at the culvert. I'll send you up four more men. If any tanks show up, get word back to me in a hurry."

"Yes, sir," Littauer said. He put into words what

the rest of the men in Charley Company were thinking. "You figure we'll join up with the rest of the outfit pretty soon, Cap'n?"

Joyce rubbed a hand across his chin with an absent
gesture. "We'll join up," he said. Far up the road, dim
in the rain, he saw a vehicle approaching, and started
to order the men down, but Littauer beat him to it.

"Under cover, you guys," he said crisply. "No
talkin'."

Joyce glanced toward him and nodded his approval
as he slipped down behind the pile of rubble, his carbine pushed forward. The vehicle came on, and presently he saw that it was a battered sedan which lurched
crazily over the road. Nothing came behind it. No
reconnaissance vehicles. No tanks. No trucked infantry. He motioned to Littauer to keep his men
where they were and stepped out into the road, carbine lifted.

The sedan creaked to a halt ten yards away at his
signal.

"Come out with your hands up," he said, and hoped
they understood English. They did.

The front door opened and a girl in overalls and
with a scarf tied around her head stepped down and

came toward Joyce through the rain. "Yank!" she said. "I'm glad to see you! I've been expecting a Red tank to pop out of the bushes at us any minute!"

Joyce dropped the muzzle of the carbine, but kept his watchfulness on him. A snub-nosed girl, he saw, with a wide mouth and a sparkle in her eyes.

"Who's in the sedan?" he asked.

"Father Dean," she said. "He's sick and old, so I brought him with me. We're the last Americans, I think, out of Taejon."

Joyce walked toward the sedan, his carbine again ready. An old man sat on the back seat. His eyes were bright and beady as he looked at Joyce. The rest of the sedan was empty.

"It's all right, Father," the girl said. "These are Yanks."

The old man stirred himself and shook his head angrily. "You've made a mess of things, young man," he said to Joyce. "You've chased me out of my house to go sky-hooting all over the country at my age. I'm too old to go sky-hooting over the country."

The girl gave Joyce a swift look and shook her head a little. "It wasn't the Americans that chased us out of Seoul, Father," she said gently. "It was the Reds. Don't you remember?"

"They're all alike. All alike," the old man mumbled. "What do they want to fight for? I've lived for seventy years and I never fought with anybody."

The girl put a hand on Joyce's sleeve and drew him a little aside. "Things get all tangled up for him sometimes. That's why I had to take care of him. Can we get south?"

Joyce shook his head. "I don't know. We're separated from the rest of our outfit. We're expecting to run into Red patrols any minute as we go south ourselves."

The girl nodded her head with swift decision. "That's the way I figured it. I'm Peg Kinley and I taught school at Seoul University before this rat race started. How are you fixed for camp followers, Private, Sergeant, General? What do I call you?"

"Frank Joyce," he said. "You'll be safer with Charley Company than you would be alone on the road. Join us if you want."

"Consider that we've joined, Frank," she said.

Joyce stood in the rain looking at her for a moment. There was a smear of mud across one cheek and the uptilt of her nose and the impudent spark in her eyes reminded him of another girl that he had known. The resemblance to Anne stopped there, he thought absently, and that was just as well. Anne would never be up here in the mud, and the things that reminded him of Anne were best forgotten.

"Wait here," he said abruptly. "I'll ride back into the town with you in a moment."

He went back to where Littauer and the two others were crouched behind the pile of rubble — noted that Henderson and the BAR had been placed where they could get a good sweep of the road, and nodded his satisfaction. Littauer was crouched at Henderson's side, spare magazines ready. O'Daniel was at the break in the fence.

"We'll go south as soon as the company gets straightened out," Joyce said to Littauer. "I'll send back word when we're ready. You'll have six men to form a rear guard . . . keep people off our backs, Littauer. If I hear shooting, we'll come back to support you."

"You won't have to come far," Littauer said, grinning. "We'll be steppin' right on your heels, Cap'n."

He spat into the mud and watched while Joyce went back to climb into the battered sedan beside the girl.

O'Daniel waited until the car had disappeared into the town; then swore in an aggrieved voice. "He can't

do that to me," he said. "Busted on the field of battle
. . . and by a such-and-such Bible thumper, at that.
It ain't legal. I'll write to my congressman."

"Bud," Littauer told him, "when you've got as
many years in as I have, you'll learn that the Army
can do anything. Just be a good boy an' maybe I'll
recommend you for a promotion."

"Nuts!" ex-Corporal O'Daniel said.

The rain had almost stopped as Joyce climbed out
of the sedan in front of the house where he had left
Lieutenant Norton. Sergeant Kruger came up to look
inquiringly at Peg Kinley, who was splashing through
the mud.

Joyce nodded toward her. "Refugees," he said. "It's
not safe for them to go south alone. We'll keep them
with us."

"Yes, sir," Sergeant Kruger said, his face noncommittal.

"How about the ammunition?"

"We're bad off," Kruger answered, and then went
on with details, but the sergeant's mind was only
partly on what he was saying.

He was wondering what bad luck would hit Charley Company next. A chaplain in command was bad
enough, Kruger thought, but now there was a woman

to take care of. And an old geezer who didn't seem to have all of his buttons. He didn't like it. He didn't like it at all.

Joyce was looking at his watch. "We'll move at sixteen hundred," he said. "Put the worst of the wounded in the jeeps and the sedan. I want a strict check made to see that we leave nobody behind."

"Yes, sir," Sergeant Kruger said resignedly.

It was four o'clock when Charley Company moved out with a point in front and Acting Corporal Littauer bringing up the rear with his six men. The rain still held off and there was a promise that the last of the sun might break through presently. After that the rain would come again — that was the way it had been for the past three weeks. One of the wounded drove the sedan and Peg Kinley splashed along in the mud beside Joyce.

She was a good marcher, he found. She marched like a man, swinging her legs in long strides. She had found a helmet somewhere, and she wore it tipped back on her head so that her dark hair fluffed out from beneath the brim. Not a pretty girl, Joyce thought absently, but an interesting one.

"I heard some of the men talking," Peg said after a little while. "You're a chaplain, aren't you?"

"Yes," Joyce told her.

"I thought chaplains didn't fight."

Joyce grinned at her — a tired grin which creased his unshaven face. "And I thought schoolteachers didn't wear tin hats and march in the mud."

"*Touché*," she said. "Someday, Kinley, you'll learn to keep your big mouth shut. You seem to wear the marks of command with a certain familiarity, Frank. That wouldn't be an accident?"

"I commanded a rifle company on Bataan," Joyce told her.

"A hard school, I've heard, Frank. How come you're a chaplain, then, when you're at home?"

Joyce grinned again. "An accident, maybe. Just say that I learned to be a powerful prayer in the Jap prison camps."

"I can see what you mean," Peg said quietly.

Behind the two of them came Charley Company, bunched tightly on the road and with the jeeps and the sedan in the middle of the column. There was little to fear from air attack, but still Joyce didn't like it as he looked back. Old habit was pushing strongly at him now, and the sight of men bunched like that bothered him. It was something like that muddy carbine that he had taken from the jeep.

"Halt the column," he said to Sergeant Kruger. "I want the company strung out more and the squads to march on either side of the road, handy to the ditches. No use to take chances."

Sergeant Kruger felt a little flicker of resentment grow in him. "Sir," he said, "the gooks haven't got any planes. The men are pretty tired an' it's harder to march off the road."

"I know," Joyce said. "Most things are hard in war. Get them off at the side. That's an order, Sergeant."

"Yes, sir," Sergeant Kruger said.

Kruger blew his whistle, halting the column, and went back. This was what came of having a chaplain in command, he thought, all of his earlier uneasiness coming back to him. He'd certainly be glad when they got back to the battalion and got another officer. If they ever got back, that was.

"March your squads on the shoulder of the road!" he called harshly. "Two squads on either side an' three yards between files! No more bunchin' up! Snap it up now!"

Ill-humored protest came from the tired men as they moved to the side of the road.

"What's this, anyway?" a voice called out, and it carried to Joyce at the head of the column. "A parade down Fifth Avenue?"

"It's orders!" Sergeant Kruger answered grimly. "You just do like you're told and never mind the griping!"

Another voice called out, "The padre must have been reading the drill regulations!"

And another voice broke in to add, "I'll take Captain Fanning for mine!"

Sergeant Kruger would take Captain Fanning, too, only Captain Fanning was dead on a ridge three days behind them. Up at the head of the column, Peg Kinley looked at Joyce covertly, curious to see how he would take that.

"They don't seem to like you much, Frank. Maybe you should have stuck to praying."

"Maybe I should have," Joyce said.

Sergeant Kruger came back and blew his whistle, and the march started again. Overhead the clouds broke away into long streamers and a sickly sun came out to put a faint warmth on the low hills. The road wandered aimlessly on ahead and there was no life in the narrowing valley except for Charley Company slogging along.

In the sedan, propped between Father Dean and a wounded soldier, Lieutenant Norton dozed fitfully. He had left Korea now and was back on the ranch in Oregon. He and his brother were going fishing this afternoon and he was having trouble finding his tackle.

"I had a Royal Coachman," he said clearly, keeping his eyes tightly closed. "Ben, you took that Royal Coachman."

Father Dean stared straight ahead, his mouth a thin line. He would certainly speak to the bishop about this when he saw him next. It was an outrage that a man his age should have to leave his comfortable study and go sky-hooting all over the country.

At the end of fifty minutes of marching, Joyce halted Charley Company for a ten-minute rest. That comforted Sergeant Kruger a little. At least it was according to the book, he thought, as he blew his whistle and swung his arm to start the column moving again at the end of the ten minutes. The sun went down behind a bank of clouds in the west and the valley was gray and cheerless once more.

. . . The three jet planes came through a notch in the hills and barreled down the valley like striking hornets.

Joyce yelled "Hit the dirt!" and heard the spatter of machine-gun bullets on the road as Charley Company spilled into the ditches on either side. He had been half expecting something like this. Such mistakes happened in war. They were things that just couldn't be helped.

The jets were gone then; far specks down the valley and winging over to come back. From the side of the road, Peg Kinley was calling, "Get down here, Frank! For God's sake, get down here! You can't do any good up there!"

The road was empty except for the jeeps and the battered sedan. Joyce started running back toward them, but time ran out on him too fast. The jets were on top of Charley Company again. Joyce threw himself flat, waiting for the hammer of machine-gun bullets.

It didn't come. The three jets went on by overhead, rocking their wings as though in apology, and Joyce knew then that the pilots had recognized them as Americans. Then the planes were gone again — back through the notch from which they had come — and he felt very lonesome all at once. Even when they had been firing, the planes had been vaguely comforting, Joyce thought. It had given him the feeling somehow that Charley Company wasn't entirely alone out here in this unfriendly land.

Sergeant Kruger came up out of the ditch, and Joyce motioned for him to follow, and the two of them went back down the length of the column, Joyce calling out to ask if anyone had been hit. It looked as though no one had, and that was lucky, Joyce thought. It is not good for tired and retreating men to be strafed by their own planes. The sedan hadn't been so fortunate. Bullets had ripped off a fender and smashed a front wheel . . . by a miracle missed the rest of the car. Father Dean still sat in the back seat, staring angrily straight ahead. Lieutenant Norton was wedged beside him, his eyes closed and his breathing heavy.

"You all right, Father?" Joyce asked.

"Sky-hooting around the country at my age!" Father Dean said testily. "The bishop shall hear about it!"

Joyce grinned and went around the sedan to where Sergeant Kruger was coming back from the tail of the column. "Anybody hurt back there?"

Kruger shook his head. "They're all okay, sir," he answered. "We were pretty lucky."

Something was puzzling Sergeant Kruger a little. By rights he ought to be feeling worse about things, he thought, what with being strafed by their own planes and all. But he wasn't feeling worse. He was feeling better. Then he finally put his finger on the reason why. It was because Cap'n Joyce had made them march on the side of the road. If it hadn't been for that, those jets would have got some of Charley Company. Probably a lot of Charley Company. By grief, it was beginning to look as though Cap'n Joyce might know something about this business after all!

Joyce said, "The sedan's done for. Put the lieutenant and the rest in the jeeps. Make room some way."

"Yes, sir," Sergeant Kruger said. "I'll make room."

Back down the column Private Ernst was poking the mud off his boots with a stick. "Now I've seen everything," he said to Kelly, the BAR man in his squad. "I have been shot at by our own planes. I'm a bloody veteran."

"Yeah," Kelly told him, spitting into the mud. "An' you were the fellah, too, that was gripin' his head off because the padre made you march at the side of the road. If you hadn't been marchin' theah you'd be a stiff by now."

"I would for a fact," Ernst said. "I certainly would for a fact. But a very good-looking stiff, Kelly."

"All stiffs are good-lookin'. Come down to Texas with me, boy, an' I'll show you some of the best-lookin' stiffs that you evah did see."

"Nope," Ernst told him. "I wouldn't want to go to Texas. I'm happy right here."

Sergeant Kruger's whistle shrilled again from the head of the column and Charley Company struggled back to its feet. The clouds were beginning to close in once more, and the dying afternoon was hot with a steamy heat. It would rain again pretty soon.

The darkness came down swiftly two hours later, and the rain came with it — a sullen, steady downpour which ran down men's necks and dripped from their chins. Joyce closed the column up now and they marched back on the surface of the road. There would be no more planes. Sergeant Kruger plodded along with his head down while doubts began to assail him again. He had never liked night marches.

Peg Kinley said, "I'll go back and march with the

jeeps. Maybe I can be of some use there," and Joyce nodded in the darkness without answering.

He had been back himself at the last halt to see how Lieutenant Norton and the rest were coming along. What he had found hadn't cheered him. The lieutenant was in a bad way; so were three of the others, but there was nothing that could be done about it now. Kalinsky had done everything for them that he could, but Kalinsky was no doctor.

At about nine o'clock the road began to bear more to the westward, leaving the rice paddies behind and climbing toward the hills. It slowed the marching column from what was already a snail's pace. Joyce wished that he had a map. He didn't. He guessed that the road was angling off to join the main highway which ran southwest from Taejon. After a while it became more twisting, and Joyce knew that they were entering the hills now. Sergeant Kruger plodded along beside him.

"We'll rest fifteen minutes instead of ten from now on, Sergeant," Joyce told him. "The company's getting pretty tuckered and we may have a fight on our hands at daylight."

"Yes, sir," Sergeant Kruger mumbled. He plodded on for a few more yards and then said, "If they send tanks after us we're done for. I guess the cap'n knows that."

"No, I don't know it, Sergeant," Joyce said. "A tank can be licked."

He didn't feel too sure about that, but he wanted to say something that would allay the sergeant's uneasiness. Actually his thoughts had been about the same as the thing Sergeant Kruger had put into words, but an officer didn't say things like that to tired men.

"We ain't licked any tanks yet," Kruger said morosely. "Cap'n Fanning got his tryin' to lick one of 'em."

"Never mind Captain Fanning," Joyce said curtly. "If they catch up to us we'll lick them. Just keep that in mind."

The lash of his voice snapped Sergeant Kruger a little out of his despondency. He said, "Yes, sir," and pulled his chin up. For a moment he almost forgot that Captain Joyce was a chaplain. Joyce was looking at his watch.

"Time for a halt," he said to Kruger. "I'm going back along the column again. If I'm not back when the rest is up, go ahead and start moving."

Sergeant Kruger blew his whistle and then stood there for a moment watching Captain Joyce's slender figure disappear into the rain. Then he sat down at the side of the road and, after a minute, folded his arms across his knees and put his head down on them while the rain seeped down his back.

Acting Corporal Littauer, marching with his six men a hundred yards behind the main body of Charley Company, heard the faint blast of the whistle signaling another halt, and waved an arm.

"Okay," he said. "Half you guys on one side of the road. Half on the other, an' keep your ears open. The gooks are apt to send a little callin' card along to us all wrapped up in armor plate."

Rube Henderson, the BAR man, sat with O'Daniel on the right-hand side of the road. Something was bothering Henderson; it had been bothering him ever since they had left the town back there in the valley. He hadn't said anything about it before, but now he put the thing into words for O'Daniel.

"I don't think that a man ought to say hard things about marriage just because it didn't work out for him, do you?" he asked O'Daniel. "Like what Littauer said back there at the culvert. Maybe he and his wife just weren't suited to each other. Now, you take Margy and me. We're —"

"Aw, for crying out loud!" O'Daniel said violently. "You and Margy go climb a tree! You ain't with Margy now! You're up here in Korea, and they'll probably bury you in one of them stinking rice paddies!"

Littauer came out of the darkness and squatted down beside them. He worried a chew off his worn plug; put it back in his pocket when they refused it.

"You birds ought to learn to chew tobacco," he said. "You ain't a soldier unless you can chew tobacco."

"You think that Bible thumper knows what he's doing up there at the head of the column?" O'Daniel asked.

"He knows," Littauer said easily. "When you know what you're doin' as well as that bird does, sonny, you'll be a soldier for sure."

"Nuts!" O'Daniel grunted skeptically. "This is a fighting outfit. I'd feel better if old Kruger was in command. At least he ain't a chaplain."

"Sonny," Littauer told him, "if Sergeant Kruger had been in command you'd probably have got a row of buttonholes stitched right up your middle when them planes come over."

"I still don't like it," O'Daniel growled. "Besides—"

Littauer stopped him with a hand on his arm as he got to his feet to listen. A faint scrape of feet was coming down the road from the direction of the column, but there was no front in this condemned war, Littauer thought, and he was taking no chances.

He pushed the safety off his rifle and called harshly, "Who's there?"

"Joyce," the voice came back to him, and Littauer relaxed. Captain Joyce came on up with the rain running down his face and dripping from the carbine he carried over his shoulder, muzzle down. He stopped close to Littauer to ask, "How does it go?"

"I've seen it go worse," Littauer told him. "It's a lousy war, though, Cap'n."

Joyce nodded. "We got away too easy," he said. "I don't like it. We haven't heard a shot fired, except from those planes, since we left the town."

"Cap'n," Littauer said, "that suits me just fine."

"It suits me, too," Joyce said absently, "but it doesn't add up. I've got an idea that as soon as daylight comes the Reds will be pushing tanks along this road fast. Better drop back another fifty yards when we start again. They may send out reconnaissance vehicles tonight. Give us all the warning you can."

"Yes, sir. We'll do that. Does the cap'n think we'll join up with the battalion pretty soon? These guys have been askin' me or I wouldn't bother the cap'n about it."

"Pretty soon, Littauer. I think it's in the cards."

Joyce fell silent for a moment. He wanted to say something more to Littauer and these men back here, but he couldn't think of exactly what words to use. "Rear-guarding a column in the face of a pursuit is a nasty job," he said finally. "Don't think that I don't know that."

"Shucks, Cap'n," Littauer said, "don't let that bother you none. We like it back here. We don't have to eat no dust."

Joyce grinned at that and lifted his hand in a faint salute as he turned back up the road in the rain. It was men like Littauer who made the backbone of armies. Rowdies and cheerful troublemakers when peace was on the world and soldiers were held in low esteem; towers of strength when the chips were down. He wished that he could have an army of Littauers.

"Big-hearted Littauer," O'Daniel said, after Joyce had disappeared into the rain. "So we love it back here, do we? We'd just love to hold off the gook tanks all day by ourselves, would we? Why don't you go jump down a well, hero?"

"Waitin' for my medal," Littauer told him. "There's the whistle, bud. Onto your flat feet, we march again."

Joyce dog-trotted along the shoulder of the road past the marching column, hurrying to get back to its head. On his left Charley Company marched silently, hunched and blurred shapes in the rain. There was no talk, and that was the surest sign that the men were dead beat. Joyce came to the break in the column where the jeeps were and slowed his pace to a walk beside the rearmost of the two. Kalinsky was plodding there with his thin shoulders hunched.

"How does it go?" Joyce asked.

Kalinsky shook his head. "Not too good, sir. We got three men in a bad way besides the lieutenant, and I ain't got no more morphine. I'm worried about the lieutenant, Captain."

"I know," Joyce said. "Don't let it get you down; you're doing a good job, son. Everything will be all right."

He went on toward the first jeep ten yards ahead, and heard a man say bitterly as he passed. "Sure.

Everything will be all right. What the hell would a chaplain know about it?"

Peg Kinley was beside the first jeep, swinging along still with her easy stride. Next to her, hanging on to the jeep with one hand, was Father Dean. The old man's mouth was bitter and his chin thrust out as he hobbled along.

Joyce said shortly, "What the devil! Why isn't he in the jeep?"

"I'm not wounded, young man," Father Dean said acidly. "There's others that are. Let them ride. If I've got to go sky-hooting around the country, I'll do it on foot."

"Let him be," Peg Kinley said in a low voice. "He's stronger than he looks. Frank, the lieutenant is getting worse."

"I know. I wish we could do something about it. We can't."

He moved closer to the jeep. Lieutenant Norton was crouched there with one of the soldiers holding him — no room for him to lie down.

"Padre," he said in a thick voice. "That you, Padre?"

"It's me," Joyce said. "Take it easy."

Lieutenant Norton was silent for a moment. It

suddenly seemed to him that it was Ben walking along beside him. But that was silly. Ben would not be up here in the rain. Ben would be back on the ranch in Oregon. Then Ben went away again, and he knew that it was the chaplain who walked there.

"It's a rough war . . . Padre," he said between his teeth. "I've got a bellyache . . . be all right as soon as I get rid of the bellyache. . . . You carry on, Padre."

"Sure," Joyce told him. "We'll all carry on, Lieutenant. Don't worry about a thing."

So much that a man wanted to do, Joyce thought as he dog-trotted on to the head of the column. So little that a man could do. War was like that — he had learned that before.

A little after midnight the rain stopped and by one o'clock the clouds had broken away again and a moon, nearly full, was shining palely across the winding road. They were deep in the hills now, Joyce saw. The going was steep and Charley Company had slowed to a crawl. He increased the rests to twenty minutes in each hour — Charley Company would get out together or not at all, he thought grimly. He had seen what had happened to men who had been left behind in the Philippines, and it wasn't pretty. No one was going to be left behind here.

Morning was coming as the road wound through a shallow saddle and then dipped down into a narrow valley where a stream came out of the hills. There was a wooden bridge down there, and a few houses on the stream's far bank. Overhead, dirty and scattered clouds mottled the sky, and mist clung to the hollows of the ground. It wasn't raining yet, but it would be pretty soon.

Joyce halted Charley Company for its rest just beyond the saddle and sat down beside Sergeant Kruger. The latter's face was drawn and pinched and his eyes seemed to have retreated far back into his head. His mouth drooped now without hope.

"We'll rest for a couple of hours on the other side of the bridge," Joyce said. "Eat what we've got left to eat."

"Yes, sir," Sergeant Kruger said dully. "Charley Company ain't got much more'n a couple of hours marchin' left in it, Cap'n. It's about run down the drain."

"Charley Company has got more left in it than it knows!" Joyce said harshly. "I don't want any more talk about it going down the drain, Kruger!"

Sergeant Kruger turned his head and surprise was on his face. Then he said, "Yes, sir," and pushed himself to his feet. "I guess I better check up on the column."

Joyce nodded and watched him go. He'd have to whip them to it, he thought, just as he had whipped Kruger to it now. That was really all that he could do for them.

Peg Kinley came through the mist then. "Morning, Frank," she said. "Sleep well?"

Joyce stayed seated while he looked up at her. Here was a woman for you, he thought, and involuntarily his thoughts went back to Anne. Anne with her petulant mouth and her pretty, wheedling ways and her selfishness. It was Anne who had driven him back to the Army, he realized suddenly, and he was grateful to her all at once for that. He might have lived all his life out without meeting a woman like Peg, if it hadn't been for Anne.

"Slept fine," he said. "It's going to be a lovely day."

Peg's eyes were bright and warm as she looked down at him; then they sobered quickly. "Frank, will we get out?"

"We'll get out," he said quietly.

"I believe you somehow, Frank. If anybody else

told me that, I'd know that they were lying. When you tell me I believe it. Why is that?"

He could, Joyce thought, say something pious about the Lord being on their side — it seemed out of place. He had never been one to put undue pressure on the Lord. He said, instead, "Charley Company is young and inexperienced, but it's tough. It will get out."

"Yes, if you take it out, Frank," Peg said softly. She crouched down beside him and placed a hand on his arm. "Charley Company would still be back in that town if you hadn't taken it out."

"How's Norton?" Joyce asked abruptly. The conversation was getting onto dangerous ground. Anyone could have taken Charley Company out, he thought.

"Pretty bad, Frank."

"A good little man," Joyce told her soberly. "It's too bad, Peg. Don't let it get you down; wars are like that."

A sudden spatter of firing came from the tail of the column, and Joyce leaped to his feet, reaching for the carbine. "Stay here," he said harshly, and sprinted back along the road to where Acting Corporal Littauer and his rear guard were posted. He was aware of the muddy, strained faces of the rest of the men as he went by.

The firing had died out as he dodged through the shelter of the brush at the side of the road and came up to Littauer's position. Littauer was there, his men fanned out on their bellies on either side of the road. Fifty yards in front, a Red soldier lay on his face in the middle of the road, and a light vehicle was disappearing around a bend.

Littauer rolled over on his side to spit as Joyce crawled up. "Reconnaissance party," he said laconically. "I think we got a couple more of 'em besides that gook in the road."

Joyce nodded. "Our running back is finished," he said quietly. "They'll send tanks as soon as that party reports. There's a stream up ahead, and we'll make our stand on the other side. You'll have to keep them off our necks until we get into position. Can do?"

Littauer spat again. "We can hold off the world."

"Move back into the saddle as soon as we clear it. It's a better position. I'll send word when you're to pull back."

"Don't worry about us, Cap'n. We're indestructible."

Joyce laid a hand on Littauer's shoulder for a moment — he suddenly was aware of a vast affection for this solid man — and then got to his feet and went on back up the road. As he passed he saw that a hard determination was beginning to come into O'Daniel's face — something that hadn't been there before. He saw the same thing in the faces of Rube Henderson and the others. They had been kids, but now they were putting their youth behind them and becoming men.

Joyce halted Charley Company in the shelter of the houses on the far side of the bridge and told Sergeant Kruger to assemble the noncoms. As he waited he took swift stock of the situation . . . not too bad a place to make a stand, he thought. The stream was a dozen yards wide and deep enough to stop tanks. The hills came down close here, and that would give them some advantage of fire. The bridge would have to be blown, but it was wooden; a rocket, carefully placed, ought to do the trick. He'd move the worst of the wounded — those who couldn't fight — up the road to where they could have some shelter from mortar fire, and leave Peg and Kalinsky and Father Dean with them.

Sergeant Kruger, his step a little more brisk than

before, came up with the noncoms, and Joyce called them over into the shelter of one of the flimsy houses. He said the same thing to them that he had told Littauer earlier.

"We're through running. A Red patrol has spotted us and their tanks will run over the top of us if we try to keep on up the road. So we'll make our stand here. Those jets spotted us last night and it's likely that we'll get some support pretty soon."

He could see the faint distrust in the eyes of the men in front of him, and he knew the reason. What did a chaplain know about fighting? That was what they were thinking. Well, he couldn't help that, but he couldn't blame the men, either.

"If we didn't have any wounded with us, we could keep on until they jumped us and then take to the hills," he went on soberly. "But we've got wounded — seriously wounded — and we're not leaving them to the Reds. We're taking care of our own."

The muddy men in front of him shuffled their feet a little and Joyce knew that he had struck a responsive chord there. An outfit takes a pride in keeping its wounded, and it takes a comfort, too, for a man likes to know that he will not be left behind should his turn come. Sergeant Johnson, who led the second squad, rubbed at his chin.

"You figure we can hold 'em off, Captain?" he asked.

"We can hold them off long enough," Joyce said. He was secretly pleased. Once, during the night, when he had stopped to ask Johnson how his squad was coming along, the latter had called him "Padre" and hadn't bothered to hide the disparagement in his voice. "Captain," now.

Joyce outlined what he wanted in curt, clipped phrases. The jeeps into cover, farther up the road. A squad to prepare the bridge for demolition. Two squads deployed on either side of the road and dug in. The rocket-launcher teams forward a little, where they could get the best field of fire. The one light machine gun that they had left placed here, and the BARs there.

Deploy. Dig in. Clear fields of fire. Harsh, precise language which the noncoms had been taught to understand. Not the language of the Church. Like Sergeant Kruger, the noncoms moved more briskly after Joyce had dismissed them. A little confidence can be a powerful tonic to harried men, Joyce thought. Kruger lingered behind.

"I miss anything, Sergeant?" Joyce asked. He knew that he hadn't, but it would make Sergeant Kruger feel good to be asked.

"Not a thing, sir," Kruger said, and there was a vast relief in his voice. "There's still enough of Charley Company left to give them a fight."

The black clouds had crawled back across the sky, and the rain had begun again as Charley Company settled down into its holes. The morning was quiet still, and Joyce was a little surprised — and grateful — that no Reds had shown up yet. He sent a messenger back to the saddle to tell Littauer to bring his patrol in, and went on up the road to where the wounded were. Peg Kinley met him.

"How are you doing, Soldier?" Joyce asked her, and her eyes lighted suddenly as she swung around to walk beside him.

"All right, Frank. Be as careful as you can when things start, won't you? Charley Company can't afford to lose you." Then she added soberly, after a moment, "Neither can I."

"I'll be careful," Joyce said absently. "How's Norton?"

"About the same. Delirious most of the time."

"We'll get help pretty soon."

"I'm sure we will, Frank."

Lieutenant Norton was lying under a tree where there was a little shelter from the rain. His face was pinched and drawn and he looked at Joyce with eyes which were seeing places other than the rain-swept hills of Korea.

"Hello, Ben," he said. "You got to leave my tackle alone, you hear? I'll beat the bejabers out of you if you don't."

Joyce squatted down and felt the lieutenant's pulse. Too fast — too fast by far. They'd have to join up with the battalion pretty quick or it would be too late for Lieutenant Norton.

"Okay, son," Joyce said gravely. "I'll let the gear alone."

"You better, Ben," Lieutenant Norton said.

The three wounded soldiers were better off. Stanwix, his leg broken, grinned tightly as Joyce squatted beside him. "Padre," he said, "you get me out of this mess an' I'll be sittin' right in the front row of your congregation for the rest of my life."

"It's a promise, Soldier," Joyce told him. Behind him, Peg's eyes were glowing as she looked down.

"You're carrying them, Frank," she said softly.

Up on the slope of the hillside, Private Ernst laid down his intrenching tool and scrambled into the hole that he had dug. "Just tryin' it on for size," he said to Kelly. "I'm finicky about my fits."

"They'll fit you for a coffin, boy," Kelly told him. "You won't be so finicky about that, I reckon."

Ernst repeated the thing that Littauer had said back there in the saddle. "Don't kid me, Kelly. I'm indestructible. I'll live forever. You ask the padre if that ain't so."

"Shuah, I'll ask the padre, sonny boy. You know, I'm beginnin' to think that padre is a sma't man."

"I been advisin' him," Ernst said.

Rube Henderson came across the bridge with four men following behind him in the rain.

Joyce met them in the shelter of one of the houses. "Where's Littauer?" he asked.

Henderson looked worried. "He and O'Daniel stayed up there, sir. Littauer said they'd stay and watch. As soon as any gooks show up, they'll come in."

Joyce nodded. He might have known that Littauer would do that. It was all right. Littauer was a hard, tough man who knew how to take care of himself. They'd go ahead and blow the bridge now . . .

couldn't take a chance on waiting until the last minute. There were too many things that might go wrong.

The bridge blew with a crash which rolled back and forth between the hills in the dreary morning. A good job. Charley Company settled down in its holes to wait. It was an hour later when Joyce, crouched where he could watch the road, heard the distant growl of tank engines. He called out, "No firing until I give the word!" and focused his field glasses on the gap in the hills across the valley.

Five minutes later, the squat silhouette of a tank lumbered into sight in the notch, and, in spite of the rainy haze, the field glasses brought it close. Men rode its top — infantrymen in the drab uniforms of the North Korean Army. It halted at the saddle's crest for a moment, the snout of its long gun sniffing the valley. A wicked and dangerous-looking machine . . .

Then, as Joyce watched, a spot of orange flame blossomed against the tank's side and the riflemen on its top spilled frantically to the ground. A second burst of flame washed the tank again as the rocket exploded; a third and smaller burst — grenade, Joyce thought — erupted in the middle of the fleeing infantrymen. They went down as though an invisible scythe had slashed at them.

Joyce said under his breath, "Good boy, Littauer," but a thread of anxiety began to run through him. Littauer and O'Daniel had waited too long up there in the saddle. It was not likely that that tank was alone.

The smoke cleared away up there and the field glasses showed Joyce crumpled bodies lying in the road like heaps of old rags. The tank was slewed around with one track ripped off and its gun tipped at a useless angle. Littauer had put his light rocket into the one vulnerable spot of those heavies — put it in at point-blank range. Then a burst of machine-gun fire came from behind the saddle, and Joyce imagined that he could see bullets chewing at the brush on the hillside as the second tank searched for Littauer and O'Daniel.

Sergeant Kruger, crouched beside Joyce, swore bitterly. "They're dead ducks," he said under his breath.

Joyce didn't answer him. The second tank came through the notch, shouldering its way past its wrecked mate, and lumbered on down into the valley. No men rode its top, but, after a little, Joyce saw them coming cautiously along behind. A few at first.

Then a heavy column of them. Halfway across the valley, the tank stopped and a man thrust his head and shoulders out of the hatch to look at the wrecked bridge; then pulled back out of sight as the tank buttoned up again. Joyce slipped down to where his two rocket-launcher teams were waiting.

"He'll come clear up to the bridge, I think," he said in a low voice. "He's not sure that we're here, and we'll wait for him. Hold your fire until I give the word, and then aim for the tracks if you can get a shot at them. I think we can knock him off the road."

The Red tank came on after a moment, moving suspiciously, but moving. Across the valley, the infantry had halted and was waiting on the sides of the road. Too far away to hurt badly yet. Joyce called back to Sergeant Kruger, sending him along the line of foxholes to caution Charley Company again not to fire until he gave the word; warn them that it would be a whistle blast and not the bazooka fire which he meant to use first.

Fifty yards from the wrecked bridge, the tank stopped again; swung its turret back and forth aimlessly for a long minute. Then the hatch opened again to let the head and shoulders of a man out, and Joyce said sharply, "See if you can get him! Then try for the tracks!"

No need for the glasses now. He crouched low in the shelter of the scrub as he heard the "whoosh" of the first rocket; the almost simultaneous crash of its explosion. Flame washed across the top of the tank and the man in the hatch was gone. Then a second rocket exploded beneath the tank's hull, slewing it around. At that range a man couldn't miss. Two more rockets smashed into the tracks, partly exposed now, and the tank veered awkwardly, limping like a crippled duck as it went over the shoulder of the road and tipped nose-down into the ditch.

Joyce said grimly, "Nice shooting, boys," and went on back up the hillside to where Sergeant Kruger waited.

Across the valley the infantry was spilling off the road, deploying on either side, and after a moment the brush swallowed the riflemen. Quiet settled over the rainy morning again.

It was ten minutes later that the first mortar shell came, bursting on the hillside above Charley Company with a wicked *spang*. A little later a heavy machine gun joined in, and Joyce heard the sharp *whick — whick* of the bullets going by over his head.

Another machine gun joined in.

Nothing to do but wait.

Sergeant Kruger, using the field glasses now, said suddenly in a choked voice, "Holy cow! It's them!"

"Who?" Joyce asked, but he knew the answer already.

"Littauer an' O'Daniel," Kruger said hopelessly. "Why didn't they stay hid? They're out there right in front of the gooks . . . off to the left of the road."

The glasses brought the two men up to Joyce, and he saw that they were coming on steadily, dodging in and out among the scattered trees which lined the road. Other men in Charley Company had spotted them now, and Joyce could hear the low murmur that was running along the line. Littauer and O'Daniel were three quarters of the way across the valley now, and, for a short moment, Joyce thought that they were going to make it; but luck was running out for them. The machine-gun fire dipped and bullets began to walk across the mud, kicking up little geysers as they came. The two men dived into the ditch and came on, crawling now.

Suspense hung over Charley Company as it watched them come. Over to Joyce's left he could hear Kelly murmuring in a steady monotone, "Keep down theah! Keep down theah!"

The ditch ran out on them a scant hundred yards from the bridge, and through the glasses Joyce could see the faces of the two plainly as they lay on their bellies and talked for a moment. Above their heads the machine gun yammered spitefully; a second joined in. Then Littauer jerked his arm in a signal and the two of them leaped up.

They zigzagged toward the bridge, running with their heads down and their feet churning the mud. Then Joyce's breath drove out in a long sigh as O'Daniel went down in a stumbling fall. Littauer spun and went back and was trying to lift O'Daniel when the bullet found him. Life went out of his legs and he sat down, then rolled onto his side. His face was plain in Joyce's glasses. Still alive, Joyce saw. Then Littauer got to his hands and knees and started to crawl on. Joyce pushed the glasses toward Sergeant Kruger.

"Hold your fire until their infantry closes in if I don't get back," he said curtly. "That's your only chance."

Sergeant Kruger said dully, "Is the cap'n —"

"Shut up!" Joyce snapped at him, "I told you that Charley Company wasn't leaving its wounded behind."

The water came to his waist as he came to the middle of the stream, and he pushed against it urgently; hauled himself up the far bank. The machine-gun fire had lifted a little now and was slamming into the hillside again. He slipped out, a fringe of bushes hiding him for the first fifty yards to where Littauer was still crawling. Then the brush ended and Joyce sucked in his breath and ran for it. He hoped that it would be a minute or two before the Reds saw him.

Littauer twisted his face into the travesty of a grin as Joyce reached him. "I'm glad to see the cap'n," he said faintly.

"O'Daniel?"

"Done for."

Joyce got Littauer across one shoulder just as the machine gun started to hammer at him. Good thing the range was so great, he thought vaguely. Lot of dispersion in those bullets, which were snapping wickedly into the mud and screaming off the road. He staggered on toward the bridge. A chance in a thousand, maybe. Maybe a chance in a hundred thousand. Well, in war a man took chances.

His luck held until almost the last. He was a scant ten feet from the stream's bank before a giant hammer slugged at his free shoulder, half spinning him about. He wobbled the last two steps and pitched head first down into the water. A half-dozen men were already there reaching for him . . . reaching for Littauer. He blacked out.

When Joyce came to, he was lying in one of the houses and Kalinsky was saying from a great distance, "The captain's sure lucky." There was a solid respect in Kalinsky's voice which was good to hear. Peg Kinley knelt on the other side.

"How about Littauer?" Joyce asked as Kalinsky tied the bandage. His shoulder and side ached with a great gout of pain.

"Awful bad, sir."

Kalinsky pulled the knot tight, and at Joyce's motion helped him to stand. For a moment Joyce thought that the blackness was going to engulf him again, but he fought it away and presently his head began to clear. Peg Kinley's shoulder was bracing him.

"Don't try to walk, Frank. We'll carry you back to where the jeeps are. Lean on me."

"I'm all right," Joyce said absently. He was listening to the *crump* of the mortar shells up there on the hillside. The tempo of their fall was faster now, and the Reds would be coming on in their assault toward the river soon, he thought. He had better get back to Charley Company now.

"Sergeant Kruger can take over," Peg was saying urgently. "You've done your job, Frank. Come on back."

"I'm all right," he told her again impatiently. Then Littauer's voice called weakly from across the room, and Joyce went over to where he lay. Pain had drawn Littauer's face into deep gullies, but his eyes were clear and steady as he looked up at Joyce.

"I wanted to say to the cap'n that it has been a pleasure to serve under him," Littauer said. "The cap'n is a soldier."

He said nothing about Joyce bringing him in. No sentimental outpourings. Joyce liked that. Liked it because he knew that Littauer had taken that for granted. Liked it because he knew that Littauer would have done the same thing and expected no thanks.

Littauer was going on now, his voice half whispering, "I would appreciate it if the cap'n would put on his other hat for a minute an' say a little something for me, sir."

Joyce stood looking down at him for a moment not quite understanding. "What other hat, Littauer?"

Littauer managed to twist his lips into his old careless grin. "His chaplain's hat, sir. I ain't ever been a great hand for prayin', but it might not do any harm now. I ain't exactly lived in such a way that I can take any chances now."

Joyce understood then, and he took off his helmet and spoke softly and from his heart. When he turned away he saw that Peg Kinley's eyes were wet; knew that his own were none too dry. Behind him, Littauer said — using Joyce's first name for the first and only time — "Much obliged, Frank," and let his breath go out in a long sigh.

Joyce went slowly back into the rain and up the hillside to where Sergeant Kruger and the rest of Charley Company waited. Sergeant Kruger's worn face lighted, showed a vast relief, as he handed back the glasses. He felt more secure, now that the captain was here.

"They're comin'," he said. "It's goin' to break loose pretty quick now."

The rain stopped early in the afternoon, but the clouds were still low and sullen. Bodies littered the road on the other side of the wrecked bridge, were scattered in the rice paddies, but still the Reds came fanatically on. There seemed to be no end to them. Charley Company had thrown them back five separate times, but it couldn't last. They would come on again, and on the sixth or seventh or eighth time they would get across the stream.

Well, they'd stick it as long as they could, Joyce thought tiredly. His shoulder burned with a red-hot flame and his ears had gone numb from the smashing explosions of the mortar shells. Charley Company was melting away fast.

Sergeant Kruger crawled up, his face masked with mud. "How many more times can we do it?" he asked dully.

"As many as we have to, Sergeant," Joyce said.

Sergeant Kruger turned and looked at Joyce, and there was embarrassment in his heavy face. "If we don't get out, I would just like for the cap'n to know . . ." Kruger began, and then his voice trailed away.

Joyce knew what this man was trying to say, and it warmed him as he rolled and stretched out his hand.

Sergeant Kruger took it with a hard grip. "I guess that that's what I was tryin' to say to the cap'n," he mumbled. Then his voice quickened suddenly. "Look, Cap'n! Over there! We got help!"

Joyce swung about to look where Kruger was pointing. Across the valley, shellfire was mushrooming up in fountains of black smoke, and men were scattering back toward the shelter of the hills. Joyce heard the sweet sound of guns coming from up the valley now. Tank guns! American tank guns!

It was a few minutes later that he heard the clatter of tank treads on the road and the racket of engines. Then a squat shape wheeled off to the side of the road down by the houses and he went to meet it. Other tanks were fanning out into firing positions on either side, and infantry in trucks came behind. Everything seemed a little blurred to Joyce, but a hard-faced, competent-looking major was talking to him.

"We'll take over. Fine job you've done. We were sent up to hold this place, but we'd have been too late if you hadn't got here first and held it for us."

It made Joyce feel good.

The battalion was assembled in a little town by a river and Charley Company joined it there. There was hot chow, and security for the moment at least. The clouds had broken away and the last of the sun was on the hills as Joyce came out of the command post. Peg Kinley was there in the street with her hair fluffing out from beneath the helmet she still wore.

"You brought them in, Frank," she said softly.

Joyce nodded, but he wasn't thinking of that. "War doesn't give a man much time," he said. "Will you marry me, Peg?"

"Of course. Did you need to ask?"

Farther down the street, Private Ernst was holding his mess kit while stew was ladled into it. Private Ernst felt good as a man that he knew in Baker Company came up to stand beside him.

"Well, well," the soldier said, "if it ain't little Willie Ernst. Heard you got lost."

"We never get lost," Ernst said. "We're indestructible."

"Heard you got a chaplain commandin' you, too. Now that's a laugh. Say us a prayer, Willie."

Private Ernst's voice got hard. "Brother," he said harshly, "we got Captain Joyce commandin' us, an' don't you forget it. I'll bust anybody in pieces that does forget it!"

Off in the shadows, Sergeant Kruger heard that and smiled to himself. Private Ernst had expressed just exactly the way he felt. Maybe everything wasn't exactly according to the book; but then, what was the book, after all?

Sky over Pyongyang

by Emile C. Schurmacher

BETWEEN the unceilinged blue sky and the mountainous Korean terrain, which at thirty thousand feet looks like smeared, yellow-brown finger-painting, you are flying your F-80 fighter bomber on the most important mission of your life.

You are Colonel Levi Chase. A group leader as well as a combat pilot, you have a lot on your mind. You fly brilliantly and alertly, yet only a part of you is concentrating on your instruments, the planes around you, the potential MIG, and other traps ahead. Most of you is anticipating the action that will take place when you reach I.P. — the Initial Point — where, according to plan, your airborne bombing is supposed to commence.

Fanning out behind you are the eighty planes of the three squadrons of your outfit, the Eighth Fighter Bomber Group, loaded with thousand-pound bombs and rockets.

"For immediate delivery in Pyongyang and never mind signing any receipts," you reflect grimly to yourself, as you automatically scan the cloudless brass-and-blue dome ahead for MIGs.

You check the position of your wing man and your fuel supply. In a fighter bomber you're forever checking fuel supply. It seems that you are always flying F-80 sorties at extreme range with just enough fuel to make it back to your base — if you're careful. And the Pyongyang operation is no exception.

This is your 357th combat mission in two wars. For months the Communists have been using Pyongyang for a buildup, somehow bringing in supplies and material despite the bridges and the locomotives you and your group have been blasting and the rails you've been cutting over and over again.

You know that up to now there has been little harassing of the North Korean capital itself. But the other day Lieutenant General Glenn O. Barcus, Commanding General of the Fifth Air Force, told you that the time had come and you nodded soberly and waited for the final briefing.

When the tacticians and the strategists, the logistics experts and the intelligence officers put it down on paper, it looked easy. On July 11, 1952, you — Colonel Chase — were to take your group over the northwest sector of Pyongyang, and knock out three all-important, primary objectives with pinpoint bombing: a roundhouse and locomotive repair plant, an ordnance manufacturing plant and adjoining ammunition dump, and a telephone and communications equipment factory.

But when you are doing interdict work and pinpointing your targets, there is a lot that the experts can't put down on paper. For one thing, they can't quite foresee the entire situation as they do with saturation bombing. And you can't leave as much to chance as when you fight air-to-air.

Interdiction has a technique all its own whether you are flying at forty-five thousand feet or at twenty-five. You may do both before your mission is completed, plus a good deal that isn't in the textbooks — as when you are interdicting a hard-to-get-at cave full of enemy, in a boxed-in canyon. Your napalm isn't going to explode at forty feet unless you've got another fighter bomber diving in behind you to machine-gun it, a neat little interdict trick developed by "Rice Paddy" Reusser and Charley Garber. But there won't be time, or room in the sky, for neat little interdict tricks on *this* mission. Or napalm, either. It is strictly a bomb-and-rocket job.

You check your fuel again. You look toward your wing men. Then forward, up and back. The group is flying in perfect formation, and by the book everything is going exactly according to plan.

It's what you expect, of course. The Eighth Fighter Bomber Group is an outfit of which you are mighty proud. And understandably you are proud of your record with it. Since taking command you have increased the sortie rate and, at the same time, cut losses by 50 per cent. This meant hard work and anxiety. Hard work you have always been used to. The anxiety came with the Korean War.

Back in the old days, you won your Air Force wings at Maxwell Field, Alabama, two months before Pearl Harbor; you trained as a fighter pilot, and got a speedy introduction to combat — in North Africa. Flying P-40 Warhawks from a sandy airstrip in Tunisia, you became the top American ace in the North

African campaign. Eight German fighters, one German dive-bomber, and one Italian fighter went down under your blazing guns; and the Nazis hated you so much that they bombed your squadron base thirty-six times before they were driven out of North Africa.

The press tried to make an incredible hero of you when you began to receive your combat medals — three Silver Stars, a Legion of Merit, five Distinguished Flying Crosses, Bronze Star, the French Croix de Guerre. But the more you went into combat — and came out of it alive — the more you realized the deadly seriousness of what you were doing. You dodged publicity as you did enemy planes, and remained the pilot least known to the public. That was the way you wanted it.

From North Africa you went to the China-Burma-India theater, where you were one of the first Air Force pilots to use napalm, a new weapon then. There in the jungle you developed a miniature interdiction campaign of your own, knocking out bridges and railroad tracks. One day a Jap bullet brought you down near Rangoon, some fifty miles inside enemy territory. Fortunately for you, a tiny L-5 liaison plane, flying from a secret base in enemy territory, picked you up and flew you to safety. Before you left the theater you got revenge by knocking down three Zeroes, bringing your score of enemy planes to thirteen.

When the war was over you left the Air Force for civilian life and went to law school for a little while. Then the Korean War broke out, and because the Air Force was still in your blood you joined up again. Eight months after returning to active duty you were flying Sabre jets over the Yalu River, and it was like beginning all over again. The planes were faster and the interdict targets were even harder to locate than those in the Burma jungle. And you were no longer a beginner.

After your first three missions you began to feel better about things, and by the time you got in fifteen missions with the 51st Fighter Interceptor Wing, you knew that you had not lost your old touch. The 51st was flying F-8os and getting a target for just about everything — from the ground with flak, in the air by MIGs, and even from snipers' hangouts on the sides of Korean mountains.

You carried on a ceaseless interdiction program, hitting everything that moves, co-ordinating napalm, bombs, .50 calibers and rockets with each mission. One day you were cutting rails, the next, fighting air-to-air. Always you were available for close support work for our ground troops or blasting enemy concentrations fifteen or twenty miles behind the Red lines.

Then you took over the Eighth Fighter Bomber Group and discovered that skillful interdiction had been a sort of warmup for this particular mission.

Minutes from the I.P., you check your fuel and frown as you look ahead in the still untroubled sky. Not a MIG in sight. It would be stupid to think the Reds didn't know that Pyongyang was about to be on the receiving end of an interdict. You are far too wise to underestimate the Commie Intelligence. The enemy probably knew when your group left its base.

He must be prepared to give you a flak reception, and you have a pretty good idea of what that will be. A few months before, when you led four fighter bombers over Pyongyang, you ran into a formidably impressive curtain of flak. The enemy has had plenty of time to reinforce it since.

"They'll probably throw up a barrage such as you've never seen before," you warned your pilots in the final group briefing back at base. "We've got to come in lower than they expect. Under the flak layer. We go out the same way."

Now, thirty seconds out of Pyongyang, the Eighth is coming in over the northwest sector according to plan, and as you make a final check and head for the I.P., you are no longer thinking ahead, but concentrating intently on the business immediately at hand. At this precise instant the enemy barrage goes into action, trying to blast your group out of the sky. They have a fairly good idea, not only of your targets, but also of the I.P. where the devastation takeoff begins. The blue sky has suddenly ceased to be blue, and is filled with smoke and exploding shells. Like a sinister curtain, the flak spreads high above the wings of the fighter bombers, then falls swiftly as though trying to ensnare them.

You grunt to yourself in satisfaction as you reach I.P. and prepare to make your own run. Your initial evasive tactic has been successful. To the last plane, the group has come in under the flak layer. The layer is lowering fast, but the F-80s are moving faster still. You hope this luck will hold. The F-80s roar in behind you in perfect co-ordination, target bound. For months, on hundreds of sorties, your group has been working on this split-second precision timing.

It had to, in order that eighty fast-flying planes might stay in the air and out of each other's way. You are flying in the world's fastest company and you are flying strictly according to schedule: your fighter bombers knock out gun emplacement A and proceed to hit position B before dealing with objective X.

There is extra heavy stuff coming up at you from the vicinity of the roundhouse and engine repair setup. It isn't the kind of target which can be camouflaged, and the enemy has made no attempt to do so. But as you go in on it and the planes behind you begin unloading their thousand-pounders, concealed antiaircraft guns around the objective go into action, throwing up a cone of fire. Your rockets seek out the guns but it is a long time before the intensity of their barrage diminishes.

You pull out and begin leveling off, and suddenly you find yourself in the midst of a lethal barrage which seems to be concentrating on you, exclusively. *This is the guy we really want*, the shells seem to scream. *This is the man we're going to get right now.*

Maybe it is just coincidence. Maybe the Commies down below are trusting to sheer luck, but the crew of one of the radar-controlled heavies has picked out your particular F-80 as the most important one to hit.

You can see the flak marching ominously across the sky. And so can your wing men, who are quick to warn you.

"Break right, Colonel; it's creeping in on you," the voice of a pilot cuts in amidst the staccato chatter of air-to-air.

You have already anticipated that, and angled away.

"That's fine. Now break right again," the pilot says.

You follow instructions as in the old days when you were a student pilot listening to your instructor through training headphones. Now the flak is jumping around and you try to anticipate the enemy gunners.

"Break left, Colonel," advises a voice. It is your other wing man. As you obey, another pilot's voice cuts in.

"What is this, a waltz?" it demands.

Fiery-fingered rockets begin reaching for the radar heavy. They close in around it just about the time that the second primary objective, the ordnance plant and ammunition dump, are hit. A pall of ugly brown-black smoke studded with tiny flashes of fire rises from the exploding ammo.

"That's doing it!" says a voice in your ear.

You recognize the voice of a young pilot. You are not quite sure whether he is impressed with his own accuracy, or with the sum total of devastation. It doesn't matter. You hear a lot of voices. A lot of swearing. The boys have to let off steam. You are breathing more easily. Some of the flak came pretty close.

The F-80s are coming through the smoke, eager to get at the third objective, the telephone and communication equipment factory.

We then proceed from primary objective B to primary objective C . . . The words of the briefing officer come back to you now as the fighter bombers roar on target. The rockets blast the antiaircraft guns with a withering barrage. Mostly they are where our Intelligence said they would be. And they are knocked out methodically, according to plan.

You soon discover that the enemy has a few surprises of his own — hidden gun positions. It seems as if two new antiaircraft guns are going into action for every one that is silenced. If anything, the flak is again increasing in intensity.

You have your fingers crossed as the thousand-pounders begin hurtling toward your third objective.

You keep them crossed as the F-80s pull out, wondering how they will be able to avoid being hit by all the upcoming stuff.

Now you have an urgent personal problem of your own. Another radar-controlled heavy has singled you out and is reaching for you. You start breaking right and left again. Smoke is billowing from the telephone plant and rising thickly from several direct hits. It is creeping upward, joining the smoke from the exploded ammunition dump, spreading an awe-inspiring blanket across the sky over Pyongyang.

The F-80s disappear into the smoke and as you hit it you are grateful for the fleeting moment of concealment. The radar heavy has lost you. Maybe it was knocked out by rockets. Maybe it is seeking another target. When you emerge from the smoke, you are headed for base. Automatically you check your fuel.

You are going to make it back.

You scan the sky. It is filled with planes — F-80 fighter bombers. You look behind you at a grim and terrible spectacle you will never forget. A curtain of flak is rising into the brown-black sky like a solid wall. It seems a miracle that any plane could pierce that wall without being shot down. In a way it was a miracle — of split-second precision and timing.

You took eighty fighter bombers in. You brought the eighty home. You went through an intense enemy barrage without major damage or the loss of a single aircraft.

That is interdiction.

The Bloodstained Beach

by Jacland Marmur

IT DOESN'T happen often. Nowadays, a car gets stalled along the roadway off the pavement, all the traffic just keeps zooming right on past. Maybe that's why he was taken by surprise. South of Oceanside, on Highway 101, he had the blue Pacific water at his back, separated from it only by a narrow beach, and small, white-headed combers were collapsing noisily upon the sand. He didn't hear these youngsters drive up in their old jalopy. With the car hood open, gray felt hat pushed off his forehead, he was growling anger at the engine. He was startled when he heard this clear, young voice so close.

"Mister," Eddie Topping said, "I know exactly how you feel. Can I help?"

The man looked up. Eddie saw he had a square,

stern face, a pale scar angling down across one temple where the close-cropped hair showed flecks of gray. It gave his eyes a piercing quality. Suddenly they smiled.

"Well, son, that's nice of you," his deep voice said. "There's a service station down the road, though. I can —"

"You let Eddie look at it. He is very good with cars." That was Susan. Tall, fine-figured girl, almost as tall as Eddie. She was walking over to them with the west wind in the tumble of her yellow hair. "Here's the tool sack, Eddie."

Susan had brought the little canvas bag. The big man saw them looking at each other for a moment. He saw Eddie grin. He saw the girl smile back, her little nose all wrinkling with her lovely smiling, telling Eddie all it meant. Seeing that, some sternness left the big man's brittle eyes. Then he heard the girl's voice, low and throaty.

"That's the ocean out there, mister, isn't it?" asked Susan. Then she gave a soft, quick chuckle. "I suppose you think that's silly if you live here. But we drove a long way to come see it for ourselves."

Eddie laughed. "That's right." He had his back turned, taking off the car's distributor cap. "We came down Highway 395. Turned off at Elsinore. Headed south on 101 at Capistrano. First time we ever saw the ocean." Eddie laughed again. "Sure is a lot of water. Pretty big puddle. I dunno."

"Eddie wants to make his mind up," explained Susan. "It's the ocean, isn't it? It's not a bay?"

The big man frowned. He appeared accustomed to swift judgment. He looked quickly toward their battered old car, parked behind his own. He saw the Kansas license plates. They weren't joking. So his frown relaxed. "Yes," he said, half smiling, "it's the ocean. Stretches all the way to China. Better than six thousand miles." He was looking straight at Susan. "Does it frighten you?"

She stared seaward, touched by wonder, seeing deep blue water flecked by runnels of white foam in the distance, glittering in brilliant sunshine.

"It's up to Eddie." Susan tossed her head. "If it don't scare him, it won't scare me."

Eddie was examining the distributor cap. "I think maybe I should join the Navy," he was saying. "That's what Susan means. Susan's got an aunt in San Diego where we're going. At a naval base like that there ought to be a lot of ships. I want to look around and make my mind up."

"Fine." The big man's steel-gray eyes showed glittering approval. "I have a son in the Marines myself. I hope you'll like the Navy."

"Like it?" Eddie was fishing for his pocketknife. "Why should I like it?" Eddie asked.

The big man frowned. "For a man who wants to join the Navy, that seems a funny attitude."

"What's funny about it?" Eddie found some emery paper in the tool sack. "Susan and I grew up together. We know what we want. We always knew. I been lucky like that. There's better ways to see the world than in the Army or the Navy. What good is it to me anyhow, seeing it alone? We'd rather see it together later, after the kids we hope to have are grown. All right, we can't. But if I —" Eddie's quiet voice broke off. "I'm through junior college," he said. "I just don't want any more deferments."

"Oh. The draft board's breathing down your neck."

Eddie straightened up. He turned round slowly. "No one's breathing down my neck!" His voice was sharp. Anger touched his dark eyes. "I'm just Eddie Topping. I'm just like a million other guys. I got a 1-A card. Okay! If that's the way things are, okay. I don't ask any special favors. But I got a right to make my own decisions!" Eddie turned his back. He was working quickly. "If we think for us the Navy would be better, then I got a right to —"

"And you mean you both drove all the way out to the Coast to make your mind up?"

"Yes. That's right." Eddie wrapped his tools. "Okay, mister. Try her out. I think she'll run." The engine purred. The big man drove a short distance on the road heel, stopped, and heard Eddie giving sound advice: "You got a cracked distributor cap. It carbonized along the split. Sent all your juice to one plug. I scraped it. Cleaned it good. Get you home all right. First chance you get, though, I'd put a new one in if I was you."

"Thanks, son. I will." From behind the wheel he looked at Eddie, and he looked at Susan. For a moment he considered offering some payment. He thought better of it right away. "I live in San Diego. Up La Mesa way," he said instead. "I know some Navy people. Maybe if I wrote a note to the captain of a fleet destroyer, you could go on board and look around. Would it help you to decide?"

"Sure," said Eddie. "I'd be thankful. Sure it would."

The big man found some paper and an envelope

in his glove compartment. He wrote rapidly, resting the sheet of paper on a magazine. He folded the letter, sealed the envelope, addressing it. Then he handed it to Eddie, saying crisply, "Stay on 101. You'll drive on past Old Town and come into Diego on Pacific. Go past the foot of Broadway on the foreshore and you'll find Fleet Landing. Here. You better write that down or you'll —"

"Oh, no, sir. It's not necessary," Susan's throaty voice said quickly. "Eddie won't forget. Eddie's got a wonderful memory. He could repeat that back right now, exactly as you said, word for word. I know."

"Fine. You ask for the duty chief in the house at the dockhead on Fleet Landing. I marked the envelope for him. He'll send you out to where the destroyer *Lockwood*'s moored." For the very first time, the big man really smiled. "I've got a pretty good memory myself, Eddie. Thanks for fixing my car." His steel-gray eyes lit up an instant. "I can't help thinking that you'll choose the Navy. I still hope you'll like it if you do."

That's how Susan and Eddie Topping came to San Diego, driving all the way from Kansas to see how the ocean looked. In San Diego they first saw the gray ships, the long, narrow fleet destroyers moored in pairs, twin gun snouts bristling. That's where Eddie first felt restless ocean water under him, first saw the knifelike bows of tin cans. Susan waited for him. She sat all alone on one of the benches at Fleet Landing with her yellow hair in sunlight, till the boat brought Eddie back. Till he came and sat beside her, taking her hand in his own.

"Did you talk it over with the captain, Eddie?" Susan asked him after silence.

"No." He shook his head, frowning. "Didn't even see him. Wasn't on board, I guess."

"You didn't get in any trouble, did you?"

"No." He shook his head again. "That fellow they call the duty chief looked at me awful funny when he read the letter. He said, 'What next!' Then he sealed the envelope again. He told me, 'Give this to the officer of the deck on the *Lockwood*, Mac,' and he sent me out there in a boat."

"What made him think your name was Mac? You didn't get seasick, did you?"

"No. The way that boat moved, it felt good. The officer looked at me funny when he read the letter too. He kept it. I guess it said he was supposed to. He

called a sailor and told him to show me around. Nice
guy. About my own age. Said he came from Brook-
lyn. He's what they call a gunner's mate. I didn't like
to ask too many questions. We should have asked that
man his name. I mean when I fixed his car."

"Yes." Only when the time for silence passed did
Susan ask him gently, "Well, Eddie, what do you
think?"

Eddie's frown grew more intense. He said at last,
"Susan, there's something terrible about them. Those
gray ships, I mean. I wish we didn't have to have
them." He turned, faintly grinning. She smiled back,
telling him again a secret, joyful thing. Eddie said,
"The men are fine."

"I telephoned Aunt Lucy. She's expecting us."
Susan understood his choice. "We better go now."

That way Eddie Topping made his own decision
for enlistment in the Navy. He learned a lot about it
after that, in boot camp, on his first destroyer duty.
Eddie learned real fast. Susan told him he looked
wonderful in dress blues. When he made his liberty in
San Diego, Susan met him at Fleet Landing. When
they walked together past the dockhead, arm in arm,
she chuckled in her throat, remembering. Eddie knew
why she was chuckling. He remembered too. He

grinned. They weren't nearly so naïve now. But Eddie's grin was just as boyish. Susan knew for her it always would be. The core of his own entity he would keep secret to all others. Not to her. It was from that place he really wrote her when the ships of his division sailed — not from Pearl, Guam or Tokyo at all.

So Eddie found out what was on the other side of all the deep blue water. And he knew what lay between. Eddie had the gift of precise memory. He could recall exactly how a man with gray-flecked temples told him the vast ocean stretched across to China. Eddie didn't get that far. Not quite. But in less than two years he knew where Korea was. And if politicians didn't know why men were backed up on a burning beachhead at a place called Hungnam in that brutal winter, how could Eddie? Eddie was a seaman first by then, quartermaster striker in the U.S.S. *James Blaney*. One of Desron 40's taut ships. She was slicing a green bow wave in the sea off Point Gaiyoto, steam feathers at her funnel lips, blowers humming, her wake uncoiling bubbles far astern toward Hamhung Bay.

Eddie was on the main deck, portside. The confused clutter of evacuation shipping was already swallowed in the land mist. But the smoking pillars hung aloft against the distant sky and he could hear the thunder of bombardment somewhere. Big stuff. Eddie was on the main deck, portside of the tin can *Blaney*, swaying easily in balance as she swung one way and then another in the ground swell, cold seas foaming past him every time she dipped. Eddie was fishing out a candy bar when the squawk box crackled at his back.

"*All hands! Attention, all hands! Hear this!*"

Eddie gave no outward sign of listening. He went on tearing off the wrapper of the candy bar. And a different voice began, distorted in the crackling.

"*This is the captain speaking,*" it said.

Eddie absently bit off a mouthful of the chocolate. Was no one paying attention at all?

"*Some people of the First Marine Division are trapped against the beach upcoast from here,*" Commander Johnson's voice went on. "*We are going to get them off. I want twelve men, all qualified in small arms. The mission is dangerous. Ensign Hartley will command the motor whaler. Those of you who wish to go will muster on the quarterdeck, starboard side. I say again: Quarterdeck, starboard side. That's all.*"

The voice and the crackling stopped. Eddie was sauntering across the thwartship passage, chewing the last of his candy bar. He didn't seem surprised to find some others there already. They had heard that crisp voice, after all.

"Well, waddaya know; here's Topping." That was little Waspy. Second hitch. Quartermaster first. "How many times I told you, Kansas? Only way to get along in the Navy is keep your ears open, your mouth shut an' never volunteer for anything."

Eddie grinned. "Only reason you're here, Waspy," he said, "the Old Man took you by surprise. I'll bet you were standing here. You're just too lazy to walk yourself over portside."

"Someone told you!" Waspy snorted. He said, "Kansas, anything the ensign forgets to put in his report, I'm counting for you to remind him. You can remember anything. Me, I —"

"Waspy means he figures he can make chief soon," Chuckland, the big gunner's mate, put in. "While you guys were logging shut-eye, me and Waspy were at the gangway when the new squadron commodore came aboard. Big four-striper, name of Lasher. I was with him in the *Lansing*. Old Whip Lasher. Waspy's

gonna show him how we do it while he flies his pen-
nant in the *Blaney*. That right, Waspy?"

"Well, anyhow," a different voice was growling,
"now I know why the exec scrounged up that life
raft we got lashed back on the fantail. We're
gonna —"

"All right, fellas; knock it off."

The bantering voices stopped at once. Watson, the
bos'n's mate, walked down the line of men. Old Navy
chief. Eyes narrow. Wisdom in them. Gig Watson
knew his trade. He turned from accurate appraisal.
They could hear him telling Ensign Hartley in a
chief's wry voice, "All heroes mustered, sir."

The officer just smiled. He looked along the row of
faces. Close behind them, where the men stood at the
rail, the green sea lifted in unsteady rhythm, turbulent
with foam caps, noisy when it fell away.

"This isn't a fishing party," Ensign Hartley said.
"Anyone can change his mind." He waited. No one
stirred. He smiled again. "I already have a radioman
for the walkie-talkie, and a pharmacist's mate. Parker
and Batley. Watson here will be with us. . . . Okay,
chief. Pick ten."

It began like that. The chief picked Waspy. He

picked Chuckland. He picked Eddie Topping too.
Eddie was one of the men who went. He wasn't glad;
he wasn't sorry. He was doing what he'd joined for.
And he would remember all of it. He had the gift of
precise memory. The tin can *Blaney* thrusting north
and east for rendezvous with men of a platoon remnant in rear-guard action, cut off from their fellows,
backed against a beach upcoast. No retreat for them
to Hungnam. Nothing but the ocean at their backs,
the ocean stretching all the way back home. Was it
just the ocean brought them to the debacle in Korea?
Eddie couldn't tell them. Eddie didn't know. If Commander Johnson did, he didn't say. He came down the
main deck, breathing vapor, glasses against his chest.
He looked the boat crew over, his cheek twitching
with fatigue.

"I want you men to understand one thing." The
skipper's voice was rasping, but somehow it had a
gentle tone. "I want you back. You are not an assault
party. Your mission is to bring those men off, the
effectives and the wounded, nothing more. If you
need fire support, you'll get it. I want you back. Every
blasted one of you! Good luck." He turned away.
"Mr. Hartley, you may prepare to launch."

It began like that. Cold mist on the water, snow on all the land peaks, barren brown hills ringing in a crescent beach. The motor whaleboat headed in toward desolation, beating out loud echoes. Eddie looked back once. Beyond the raft they towed he saw the ship, destroyer U.S.S. *James Blaney*, rocking in the land swell, small foam feather at her bows. She loomed up long and narrow, dark shapes in her bridge wing, gun mounts of main battery all snouting at the shore. Then the whaleboat grounded. He could hear Gig Watson growling as the men leaped out, the whaleboat backing off.

It went easy. Easy landing. Lucky, maybe. All hands took cover by the briefing orders. Eddie crouched behind a boulder next to Waspy. Chuckland over there, his submachine gun ready in big paws. And all the darting eyes on Ensign Hartley, murmuring to Parker. Parker at the walkie-talkie, droning, "*Butterball; hello, Butterball. This is Mudhen. Shoreside now. No enemy reaction. How do you receive me? Over.*"

Then the whistle, shattering taut stillness. Three sharp blasts. All the eyes snapped round. And a harsh voice snarling blasphemy from somewhere, "Where you mudhens been? What kep' you? Sergeant Risko here. Sound off, someone, or I —"

"Here, Sergeant." Ensign Hartley showed himself. "Over here. Are you in command of the platoon?"

The shape appeared from nowhere. It came swaying across broken ground, automatic weapon in its hand. Not walking. Staggering. Eyes hollow in a grizzled face of bleak exhaustion framed by a grimy parka hood. Eddie had never seen a look like that before on the face of any man. Sergeant Risko, 1st Marines.

"Let's get out of here," his voice was croaking. "We got fourteen wounded. If that's what you want to call it. Ten of 'em can walk. Gimme some men to help." He pointed. "You see what's left of that fishing village in the gully up there? That's where the lieutenant is. Machine-gun emplacement. Enfilades the whole approach. Gook patrol comes screaming at it every day. Let's get out of here before they try again. The lieutenant says he won't leave there till all the men withdraw."

It went like that. Still no reaction. How long could luck hold? Eddie remembered Sergeant Risko's face. The others looked the same. How else would combat people on a beachhead look? The landing party fanned out. Risko told them where. The remnant of the 1st platoon was gathering back where surf curled. And Parker at the walkie-talkie, passing Ensign Hartley's words, telling Butterball about it. Not how men looked. Not what they endured.

"*Butterball, this is Mudhen. Can you see the broken buildings of that village? Bearing from you about nine-oh-relative. In the gully mouth. Request main director on it. Target area will be beyond it yards one-double-oh. I say again: Beyond it yards one-double-oh. We may need fire there. Acknowledge. Please stand by.*"

That's what Eddie Topping heard. On the distant water U.S.S. *James Blaney* loomed in sea haze, misty tatters at her signal yard. The twin mounts slewed, the gun snouts elevating all in unison. They hesitated, crawled down, stopped. Shoreward, luck still held. Till then. Then luck ran out. A cracking carbine splattered it apart.

Instantly, beyond the gully mouth, the screaming started, the weird banshee howling Sergeant Risko had spoken of, the rattling fire of small arms. Eddie spun around in time to see quick-licking tongue-bursts answer from the lieutenant's MG emplacement in the rubble heap. He saw shapes darting toward it, stumbling, falling. Grenades exploded in the ruin.

And it burned. Three men were running from it now, doubled over, racing for the beach. Eddie heard the sergeant's hoarse voice, the chattering of weapons all around him. Fire to cover two exhausted men and the platoon lieutenant. Not enough. Not near enough. One spun and fell. Another dropped and crawled for cover, and the third dived headlong at a boulder.

"Butterball, this is Mudhen. Commence firing. Urgent. Commence, commence, commence. Butterball, this is —"

Eddie leaped up. He didn't know why. He just knew he had to. He was racing forward over broken ground, darting to one side and then another, seeing nothing but a boulder where he knew a man lay. He heard Ensign Hartley shouting at him. He heard Sergeant Risko too. Eddie never stopped. He couldn't. Till he stumbled, fell. Close enough, though. He could see lieutenant's bars, a pain-racked, stubble-bearded face and hollow eyes. Eddie crawled there. The haggard eyes tried hard to grin.

"You sure tried, Sailor."

"Take it easy now, Lieutenant. Salvos coming from the *Blaney*. She'll —"

Seaward, flame spears leaped from *Blaney*'s guns. They ripped the mist apart, roaring thunder. Beyond the village rubble, earth exploded, debris splattering aloft. The lieutenant made it now; he really grinned. "Half hour too late," he said. "For me, I mean." Eddie saw the red stain spreading on his chest. "Listen, Sailor. Urgent information for your CO. You got something you can write on?"

"No, sir. Say it. I'll remember. Say it. I remember good."

"Maps, co-ordinates, all gone. I laid it out in ranges and cross bearings. Should have given it to Risko. Couldn't. Gave it to the corporal and to Lingman. Dead. Both —" Thunder roared again. Second salvo out of *Blaney*. The lieutenant's gasping voice went on, "Enemy ammo dump. Bearing from the peak of Mount Sontoku three-two-eight. Range two-three-double-oh. Bearing from the peak of Hill Teikumishan . . ." Third salvo from the *Blaney*. Ensign Hartley spotting, closing down the range. And Eddie listened, deeply frowning. The words and figures lodged in Eddie's mind. Sealed in a corner of his brain, when Eddie called for them they'd be there. "Those camouflaged ammo and supply dumps are in range of your ship's guns. I hope you —"

"Don't you worry, sir. I'll give it to the skipper."

"I doubt it, Sailor. But okay. You tried. Push off."

"It's not far, Lieutenant. Easy now. I'll carry you."

"I said push off! I've had it. Shove off, Sailor! That's an order."

"Sorry, sir." Eddie's voice was solemn. "This here's an amphib operation. I'm not under your command."

The rest compacted. Eddie thought it happened quickly, but it didn't. Underfoot the ground kept surging with concussion. Tongues of orange lightning in the sea mist. U.S.S. *James Blaney* shooting. Fire cover for poor devils on a beachhead. Eddie thought he heard men shouting. He kept staggering beneath his heavy burden. All he wanted was to reach the place where surf curled. How much farther? They ought to stop their shouting at him. Whose voice was it? Waspy's? Was it Chuckland? Then he recognized the hoarseness, recognized the bitter tone. It reached him like a sorrow, like a mourning for a great deal more than a platoon commander.

"Put him down, kid." It was Risko's voice. "The lieutenant's dead," the voice snarled flatly. "Put him down, I said!"

"I tried." What else could Eddie say. "I wanted him to live. I never wanted anything so bad." It was going round in Eddie's brain. Like a questioning of wasted glory, maybe. Like a questioning of wasted pain. "I tried," he said to Ensign Hartley in the whaleboat too.

The officer spoke harshly to him, with abruptness, like the hard, cold slap of reprimand. Combat shock. Mr. Hartley recognized it. Eddie quieted at once. The ensign knew he would. Eddie must have told him how he had to see the skipper, must have told him why. Eddie saw the officer's quick nod. He knew the guns were silent now. He saw the faces of the wounded in the boat, the others on the towing raft. Grizzled faces, stamped with bleak exhaustion. And the gray hull of the *Blaney* looming close, men peering down along the rail, the scrambling nets awash. He remembered Sergeant Risko worrying about his men, snarling at them as they stumbled to the *Blaney's* deck, rescued remnant of a full platoon. Thirty-eight, no more.

The next thing Eddie knew, he was in the skipper's sea room. Never would have made it up the ladders without Watson's help. The chief was telling Commander Johnson who the kid was, what a fool thing he'd done. Didn't have sense enough to know how burp guns cut men down. Shot with luck. Carried the lieutenant all the way back to the beach. The lieu-

tenant didn't have a sailor's luck, though. Had to leave
him. He was dead. Gave Topping urgent oral information while he could. Topping was here to
report.

There was another officer beside the skipper there.
Big man. Big four-striper. Cap-peak ridged with
scrambled eggs. That would be the squadron commodore. Captain Lasher. Old Whip Lasher. His
square face danced somewhere far in Eddie's mind.
No time. Not now. Commander Johnson, seeing
Eddie's face, pushed out the door. His voice cracked
to the bridge wing, "Coffee! Hot! Hot coffee here!"

The skipper held a wardroom cup to Eddie's lips.
Eddie gulped a scalding mouthful. "Please, sir," he
said. "Please, sir, write it down. I don't think I could
say it more than once."

Eddie was reaching back to sealed compartments
of his memory, fiercely frowning, ordering his small
gift to release what he had stored there. Nothing!
Panic seized him. There was nothing there! Then all
at once he thought of Susan. The core of him grew
quiet. Eddie stared out at the middle space of a tin
can's narrow sea room off Korea, seeing Susan's smile.

And the compartment opened for him. He was
talking in a monotone, thinking all the time of better

things. "Those camouflaged ammo and supply dumps are in range of your ship's guns." He began repeating bearings, ranges — words — like a litany — each one precise, exact. They came from where he'd put them. Chief Watson wrote them down. "Listen, Sailor," Eddie droned. "Enemy ammo dump. Bearing from the peak of Mount Sontoku three-two-eight. Range two-three-double-oh. Bearing from the peak of Hill Teikumishan . . ."

Eddie never stumbled. He went on until the end. Then he stood there, drained and empty. Skipper and the chief both gone. Commander Johnson and the navigator were triangulating bearings, plotting targets on the chart. The gun boss was suggesting courses that would bring his twin 5-inchers on the range. Eddie thought he was alone there in the sea room. Only for a moment. Only till the deep voice spoke.

"Well done, Topping," it was saying. And the voice went on, "I took your advice. I had a new distributor cap installed." Eddie looked up quickly, startled. Now he knew! He recognized the square face, scar along one temple, stern eyes faintly smiling. "I have a good memory myself, son," he heard Captain Lasher say. "Did you get on board the *Lockwood*, back in Diego?"

"Yes, sir. But I never knew —"

"Of course not. The letter expressly said you were not to be told who sent you." The narrow, piercing eyes were really smiling. "How is Susan, son?"

"There are two Susans now, sir," Eddie blurted, and his face began to glow. "One of them I've never seen yet. Weighs twelve pounds already. We — They" — he broke off — "they're both fine."

"I'm glad. I'm glad you chose the Navy too. I thought you would. I hope you like it, son?"

Eddie did his best to stand erectly at attention. Like it? He had never judged it that way. Behind his mind, behind the weariness, behind the silent instant there were things lodged he would not forget. Not ever! Tin can crashing in a seaway. Tropic thunder on the water and the thresh of deep-sea rain. Guns of Hungnam. Scream of aircraft. Faces of the combat people, battle-scarred and empty on a beachhead of Korea. Face of a Marine lieutenant dying. Like it? What could Eddie Topping say?

"The choice was mine, sir." Eddie knew you had to answer four stripes. Eddie knew free choice was precious, fragile, the last best thing men could have. "I don't regret it, sir," he said.

He turned away. The sea-room door pulled open.

Skipper coming back, eyes taut with strain. Eddie saw winter twilight glinting on a running sea crest. Night already? It astonished him.

And at his back he heard Commander Johnson telling Captain Lasher: "I've been talking, sir, with Sergeant Risko. The commanding officer of his platoon . . ." Quick silence. Then the skipper's voice again, the slow voice saying: "The lieutenant's name was Lasher, sir. Lieutenant Clifford Lasher. I — I'm desperately sorry."

And then stillness. Stillness in the sea noise, in the cluttering of wind past signal halyards. Eddie spun around. One foot across the weather sill, he stood there wide-eyed, staring back. What would a man's face look like in such stillness when his son died? Bleak face. Face of sorrow. Face with eyes unseeing. Eddie's lips were parted. Speech was in his throat. He felt compelled to utter grief's thin fellowship. In officers' country? What could Eddie say? He stifled speech in time. He let the door close quietly. He went away.

So U.S.S. *James Blaney* steamed in darkness. Taut ship. Buttoned up. Coming on the charted range. Skipper in the bridge wing, close against the thin steel windbreak, alert talker near him. Captain Lasher stood there, too, his face a cold, pale mask. Words clamored in him. If he didn't say a different thing, a needless thing, he'd be defenseless, naked. So his deep voice rumbled to the skipper of the *Blaney*.

"I must tell you, sometime, how that lad joined up. Remind me. I mean Topping, that seaman first." Captain Lasher's voice was toneless. Words like that were never meant for answer. Fragile mantle against sorrow, nothing more. Presently the toneless voice went on, "He'd rather be back home in Kansas. Lots of them like that. And they ship over. They make fine men too. It's odd, Bert, odd."

Then the firing buzzer sounded. At his battle station, Eddie heard it, heard the twin 5-inchers thunder. Steady salvos. Walking HE shellfire back and forth along dark shore hills of Korea. Flaming fingers searching for a dead lieutenant's target. When the guns flashed they revealed dark lumps of running sea an instant, patches of the *Blaney*'s tipping deck. Eddie saw eruption on the distant land. Pillar of enormous flame against the night.

Found the ammo dump!

Eddie felt a cold elation. But the core of him was

quiet. Turmoil or bombardment couldn't reach it. Nothing could.

Nothing except Susan. She was always there. Susan wouldn't have to wonder about Eddie's choice or judgment. Susan knew he asked no special favors. He was like a million other guys. Whenever folly, blunder, wasted power, brought again the need for them, they came. They came to oceans they had never seen before. They came from Iowa and Oregon. From Kansas too. They did what they were called to do. The best they could, they did it. Liking it or not, they did it. Susan wouldn't have to ask him. Susan knew.

Heroes Don't Sound Off

by William Chamberlain

Requirements for admission to the United States Military Academy at West Point are stern and immutable. One such requirement states: ". . . an applicant shall have reached his seventeenth but not his twenty-second birthday on the date of admission." Joe Andrade made it barely by the skin of his teeth. He celebrated his twenty-second birthday just a week after he had put on his first plebe gray.

As a matter of course, Joe would be "Dad" to the rest of his classmates. Not that that bothered him. He had a sense of humor that went with his homely face and his red hair, and he didn't bother easily. That was just as well, because it was a rough road that had finally brought Joe there to the austere school on the Hudson. At a time when most of his classmates had still been going to high school, playing football and dating girls, Joe had been learning of war in Korea. It had been at a place called Mincemeat Ridge that the West Point road had begun.

Just after dark, Able Company — reinforced with two machine-gun squads from Dog, the heavy-weapons company of the battalion — had left the MLR along Mincemeat Ridge to take its turn at outpost duty. Able had marched glum and unhappy — for the grapevine, accurate in these matters, had it that the Chinese meant to attack during this period of the full moon. Nobody was enchanted with the prospect of a fight, when a truce might come up from Panmunjom any day now.

From Mincemeat a subridge poked a finger down into the valley to where a knob, known as Harry's Hat, had been trenched and bunkered and wired-in as an outpost uncomfortably close to the enemy positions which glowered down from across the way. Four hundred yards in front of Harry's Hat was a still lower knob, dubbed Land of Jubilee by some unknown poet, which formed an outpost to the outpost. To Jubilee went Sergeant Joe Andrade with his heavy-machine-gun squad. His mission was to support Able's second platoon garrisoning the place.

It was a little before 2300 — the night clear and the

moon full — when Lieutenant McGraw came into the bunker where Joe had his heavy water-cooled .30 sited to shoot down into the valley. McGraw was an artilleryman — new out here — who'd come up front tonight to see what the place was like. It was a fool thing to do.

He said now, "Evening, Sergeant. How's it going?"

Joe answered absently, "Okay, Lieutenant," and finished checking the belt feed pawl on the .30. He slammed the cover down and yanked twice on the bolt handle and saw the belt jerk forward as the block slammed home. Beyond the embrasure the valley lay white in the moonlight, empty except for tree stumps showing sad as the snags in an old man's senile smile. Joe squeezed off a short burst and the gun stuttered its ghoulish laughter into the night.

"She's okay now, Benny," Joe grunted, and straightened out of the way. "Take her over, boy."

Joe had been out here two years now, and nights like this were an old story to him. He was lanky and whipcord-tough and he had a homely face and big ears and freckles. People instinctively liked Joe.

McGraw asked, "How's for a look?" and was moving toward the embrasure when the grenade came through as the Chinese attack hit Jubilee.

Benny yelled, "The Chinks are sproutin' out of the

ground —" and then the crash of the explosion cut his words off.

He must have been out for quite a while, Joe was thinking as consciousness crept back into him. The first thing that he noticed was that the poncho was gone from the door of the bunker, so that moonlight streamed in. After a while he crawled over to look out. Nothing moved on Jubilee, but he could hear firing in the direction of Harry's Hat. He went back toward the gun — one of the tripod legs was bent so that the gun, bulky in its water jacket, was canted up at an angle. Blood dripped from a gash in his face and Joe wiped it away. As he got the dirt out of his eyes he saw that Chinese were climbing toward him.

He found a sandbag, rolling Benny out of the way to get at it, because Benny was dead. Everybody in the bunker was dead except himself, Joe guessed, as he tried to wedge the bag beneath the tripod's bent leg. He didn't have much luck and the Chinks were getting closer. They moved boldly in the moonlight, believing Jubilee knocked out.

A voice behind Joe said, "Give me a hand. One of my legs is no good, but prop me against the wall and I can help."

It was McGraw, and Joe was glad to see him. They

leveled the gun until Joe could get the Chinese in his sights. He pressed the trigger, and the heavy .30 made a noise like a small boy dragging a stick along a picket fence. The Chinese melted into the ground.

"You have such interesting evenings in the infantry," McGraw said vaguely. "Is it always like this, Sergeant?"

Joe didn't like the high note in McGraw's voice. The officer was hit pretty bad — you could see that from the way his eyes had retreated into his head.

"Let me have a look at that leg of yours while we've got a minute," Joe said, and left the gun.

"What's with the rest of everybody?" McGraw mumbled, stumbling over his words. "We here on Jubilee alone?"

"Looks that way," Joe told him. "Take it easy."

The leg was bad and McGraw wouldn't leave here under his own power, Joe saw grimly. No time to worry over that now, though, because the Chinks were coming on again. He could see them skulking through the scrub and he could hear the eerie *beep* of shepherds' pipes as they signaled. The heavy .30 took up its sharp, stuttering racket again. McGraw, propped against the wall, fed belts until he passed out, and after that Joe worked the gun alone. Then a bullet punctured the water jacket and the gun jammed as its barrel glowed red-hot. Chinese were swarming over Jubilee like angry hornets as Joe moved to the bunker door and methodically began to pitch grenades.

"We could sure use some of your artillery right now, Lieutenant," he said — not that he thought that McGraw could hear.

McGraw did hear. "Had a signal pistol somewhere," he mumbled vaguely. "Shoot flare . . . call for VT fire."

Joe knew what VT fire was. Artillery shells, proximity-fused, would shower down an iron hail on Jubilee. Hot metal would sweep the knob clean. It could be that Joe and McGraw would get clobbered, too, despite the bunker. Joe didn't care; he wanted the Chinks. He searched on hands and knees and found the pistol. Got back to the door.

"Here goes nothing," he said, and fired.

On Harry's Hat, the artillery FO saw the flare, spoke cryptic words into his radio and presently the VT — proximity-fused — fire came down on Jubilee. Joe heard its iron patter on the bunker's roof. Beyond the door he could see dust dance beneath its flail. Screams and a confused yelling mingled with the dull *varoom* of the explosions. When the yelling stopped, Joe crawled back to the door; he looked out and fired a second flare and, after a little, the fire lifted.

"We got to get out of here," he said thoughtfully.

McGraw answered, slurring his words, "No good, Sergeant. You go. Leave me here. That's an order."

"I'm deaf," Joe told him dispassionately.

He got McGraw out of the bunker and onto his shoulders. Chinese artillery fire was falling in the saddle between Harry's Hat and Jubilee now. No help for it, Joe thought; they'd take their chances. He started back with the shellbursts opening like evil flowers ahead and on either side of him.

He was halfway through the saddle when three Chinese rose out of the ruined communications trench to fire at him with burp guns. Joe heard the zip of the bullets as he fell flat. He killed the three with his carbine and then hoisted McGraw back onto his shoulders and went on once more.

It seemed a long while later before he saw people from Harry's Hat coming to help. And it wasn't until he was in the aid station that Joe found that he had a couple of broken ribs and a bullet through his shoulder in addition to his cheek laid open to the bone. Mc-

Graw had been hit again, too, but Joe had brought him in alive.

Joe was in the hospital when the truce came a few weeks later. Then one afternoon McGraw gimped into Joe's ward on crutches and stood with a big grin while a general pinned the Silver Star and Purple Heart to the front of Joe's pajamas. McGraw lingered, sitting on the edge of Joe's bed, after the high brass had gone.

"In my book they don't build medals big enough for guys like you, Joe," he said thoughtfully, twisting the West Point ring on his finger. "The odds were a hundred to one against you getting back alive with me riding your back. Why did you do it?"

Joe thought of that, scowling a little. "I guess it's just that a man takes care of his own, Lieutenant," he said finally and then grinned. "You were my loader, weren't you?"

McGraw nodded soberly. "My old man was killed at Salerno, Joe," he said. "He was the best officer I ever saw, and that's what he always used to tell me: 'The mark of a good officer is that he looks after his own.' Have you ever thought about going to West Point, Joe?"

Joe shrugged. "I used to think about it when I was

a kid on my old man's fishing boat in San Francisco,"
he said. "The old man laughed at me. He said West
Point was for rich men's kids."

"He was wrong," McGraw said earnestly. "You've
still got time — the Army will send you back to West
Point prep school to try for an appointment, if you
ask. How about it?"

Unconsciously, Joe lifted a hand to touch the bits
of metal and enamel on his chest. Then he looked at
the ring on a finger of McGraw's left hand and made
up his mind. Those kid dreams, that he had discarded,
came back with a new shininess now.

"Thanks, Lieutenant," he said quietly. "I'll do it."

So, on a blistering July day, Joe Andrade climbed
the hill from the West Shore station with a hundred
others who would be his classmates, and the gates of
West Point opened to take them in.

He sweated plebe year out — was still around after
the foundlings, classmates who had failed to make the
grade, had marched sorrowfully back down the hill in
January and June. He never mentioned his service in
Korea, although everyone knew that he had come to
West Point from the Army — he'd been wearing the
Army's khaki when he'd arrived. His Silver Star and

Purple Heart stayed in his locker in the trunk room; no cadet would learn of them from Joe Andrade's lips.

Upper classmen liked Joe because he was a good plebe — cheerful and quick to learn, and a snappy soldier. His classmates liked him because he didn't try to use his previous military experience to "bone files" — advance himself — at their expense. They called him "Dad" and inquired solicitously after his gray hairs and his "rheumatiz," and tried to imitate his way of taking things. Not that Joe didn't have his share of troubles. Even in his plebe year he had acquired a reputation for breaking regulations in original and bizarre ways.

At the beginning of his third year at the Point, Joe was made a cadet corporal, but it didn't last long. Just after Thanksgiving of that year he was received into a select company known in cadet parlance as "BA-AB" — short for "busted aristocrat and area bird" — when he ventured forth on a midnight expedition after taps and got caught. The fact that such well-known characters as George Armstrong Custer and one named Ike had been guilty of similar peccadilloes didn't save Joe. He lost his corporal's stripes and was sentenced to walk the area for four months. He accepted his fate cheerfully.

It wasn't until April of his last year that a couple of events came along that really shook Joe. The first was when he met Sue Holly at a hop and fell in love. It was just unfortunate that Stan Holcomb should have been dragging Sue at the time. Stan was a cadet captain — he commanded one of the companies in the other regiment — and he had a pretty good opinion of himself. He'd been pretty stuffy about Joe cutting in at the hop. Later, when Sue had taken to coming to the hops with Joe instead, Stan had taken it as a personal affront.

It wasn't long after that when Joe was summoned to his company orderly room and the roof really fell in on him. Captain Murphy, his Tac — the Regular Army officer in charge of the company — was waiting for him. Joe turned out a snappy salute and said, "Sir, Cadet Andrade reporting as ordered," and wondered what it was all about.

"I have news for you, Mr. Andrade," Captain Murphy said. "The period of penance for your after-taps activities having expired, I am happy to tell you that on Saturday you will be promoted to cadet sergeant. Orders will issue shortly to that effect."

"Thank you, sir," Joe said with a big grin.

"You can wipe that grin off, Mr. Andrade," the

Tac said in a flat voice. "You haven't heard all of it yet. Also, effective Saturday, you will be transferred to a corresponding company in the other regiment, that company having a vacancy for a sergeant. As you no doubt know, this company does not have such a vacancy."

For a moment Joe stared back. Then a faintly horrified expression settled into his face. "If I've got to be transferred, to be a sergeant, I'd rather stay a private, sir," he said stubbornly. "This is my company. I don't want to leave it."

Captain Murphy had been a cadet, and he knew how Joe felt. Companies in the Corps are close-knit corporations, and it is not an easy thing to leave the associations you have known for almost four years and fare forth among strangers.

"The Army, Mr. Andrade," he said severely, "does not ask a man where he *wishes* to go — it simply sends him there. On Saturday afternoon you will move to your new company and report yourself for duty to Cadet Captain Holcomb, who commands same. Any questions?"

It wasn't until then that the full extent of the disaster which had befallen him dawned on Joe. Good grief! he thought. Stan the Military Man's company!

Andrade, you're a dead duck! He made his face wooden as he mentioned something of that to Captain Murphy.

"Sir, if I've got to be transferred couldn't I go to some other company than the one that Cadet Holcomb commands? The captain knows that I've got only twenty-eight demerits left to last me until June. I've just got a feeling that —"

"Mr. Andrade," Captain Murphy said, "I am familiar with your demerit record — I consider that it took a touch of genius on your part to compile such a record. You do not go in for the lesser crimes such as 'late at chapel formation' or 'dust on rifle at Saturday inspection,' do you, Mr. Andrade?"

"No, sir," Joe said, keeping his face wooden.

"Your lapses from grace," Captain Murphy went on thoughtfully, "are more spectacular — and more expensive in demerits. Last month you were reported for marching a detail to the gym at a Prussian goosestep. The month before you were in the glue for some interesting experiments in missile ballistics performed in the Ordnance lab. What I am getting at is that your demerit record — which is disgraceful — is something that you have brought upon yourself. You will have to solve it for yourself, if you mean to graduate. I assume you want to graduate?"

"Yes, sir," Joe said soberly now. "I want to graduate."

Captain Murphy was silent for a moment — then he went on in a flat voice: "It could well be that you and Cadet Holcomb will be good for each other, Mr. Andrade. You throw the book away. Mr. Holcomb, I understand, holds the book sacred. You are both partly right and partly wrong. I hope that the two of you will make some important readjustments between now and June. That is all, Mr. Andrade."

The order appointing him a sergeant in the Corps of Cadets was published on Friday, and on Saturday afternoon Joe moved to his new barracks. He was arranging his gear in his locker — talking with Chubby King, one of his new roommates — when Stan Holcomb walked into the room. The latter was a slim, good-looking cadet, but arrogance gave his face a faintly sulky expression, and his eyes were unfriendly.

"So you've moved in, Andrade," he said abruptly to Joe. "You should have reported to me first — or didn't they teach you military courtesy when you used to be in the Army?"

Joe went on stowing clothes in his locker, but his

eyes narrowed a little. That was a pretty thinly disguised crack to remind him that he'd once been an enlisted man, he thought. Stan Holcomb had gotten his pre-West Point training in an expensive military prep school and he didn't intend that Joe should forget that he was a big wheel around here. *Whoa up, Joe. Take it easy. You've got to live with this guy for the next couple of months and you've only got twenty-eight demerits left. Remember?* He shrugged and turned.

"Shucks, I was just a yardbird when I was in the Army," he said mildly. "Nobody told me anything, pal."

Holcomb looked down his nose. "I can believe that," he said in an unpleasant voice. "We may as well understand each other, Andrade. I'm responsible for this company. I don't intend to have some stranger come in here and foul it up — get me in the glue. You step out of line and I'll report you. Is that quite clear?"

"Don't beat on me, Cap," Joe murmured. "I'll be good."

A flush crept up into Holcomb's face. "I won't tell you again, Andrade. Just watch your step!"

"I'll tippy-toe," Joe said, hanging onto his temper. "Now, suppose you get out of here and let me brood."

Holcomb went, and for a moment Joe stared thoughtfully after him. Then he turned back to where Chubby King was slouched in a chair, his feet on the table. Chubby was first sergeant of the company — a happy-go-lucky character from Texas.

"He always like that?" Joe wanted to know.

"Yup," King grunted, unmoved. "He's military. Veddy, veddy military. You want to watch out for him. Especially as it seems as how there's a rumor around that you up and stole his gal."

"I didn't steal her," Joe growled. "She came down on a blind date from school and drew him — is it my fault if Sue prefers a warm, friendly ex-enlisted type to a noble captain type who stands around waiting to be admired? His blood's on his own shirtfront."

"Just be careful none of that blood don't get rubbed off on you, dear," King said, grinning. "Our Stanton Melrose Holcomb can be an awful fast man with a pencil and a quill pad."

Joe found that out. On Sunday, Holcomb reported him for shoes not properly shined, talking in ranks and unmilitary bearing at chapel formation.

One day in his new company, and his demerit margin had already started to melt away at an alarming rate, Joe thought grimly that night. It was pretty plain that he had better drive with a tight rein from here on in if he didn't want four years of sweat — and his dreams of a lieutenant's bars — to go down the drain.

Joe came up to the last Saturday before June Week with just six demerits left — he'd been hoarding them like diamonds and pearls, and he should make it now, he was thinking, as he stood in the area in the May sunshine waiting for the company to be dismissed. Inspection was over and the freedom of the weekend lay ahead. Already the nearness of graduation had started a heady excitement running here among the gray cloisters on the plain above the Hudson.

Joe could feel that excitement — a good feeling as he looked toward the east sally port out of the corners of his eyes. A knot of visitors waited there — cadets' girls with their dresses making a bright splash of color in the afternoon. Sue had come down for the hop, and Joe's pulses jumped a little as he saw her, standing a little apart from the rest. She was tiny, with a piquant face and laughing eyes, and Joe had made very special plans for this afternoon. They'd go down Flirtation Walk to a shady spot close to the river . . .

Stan Holcomb's cold voice cut into Joe's thoughts with its irritating authority. "Andrade, report to me in my room as soon as the company is dismissed. First sergeant, dismiss the company!"

There was the clash of bolts as the company executed inspection arms and then Chubby King said, "Dismissed!" in his lazy Texas voice, and the ranks melted into noisy groups streaming toward the barracks steps. Chubby fell into step beside Joe.

"What's with Stan the Military Man now, Joe?" he asked, not bothering to keep his voice down. "You done something to him or he just mad because the beauteous Suzy waitin' for you?"

Joe shrugged. "Probably just wants to chew on me a little to keep his teeth in shape," he murmured. "He didn't skin me at inspection — I've got nothing to worry about."

Joe was worried, though. He didn't kid himself — if anything should happen to put him over in demerits he wouldn't graduate, period.

Stan's two roommates were hurriedly changing into dress gray when Joe reached the room. He sat on a corner of a table and talked idly while he waited for Holcomb to come. The two left and another ten minutes ticked by and Joe thought impatiently of Sue waiting for him down there by the sally port.

Holcomb came then. He moved across the room and stood behind his study table with no apology for his lateness. Joe put a rein on his temper as he looked back at the other through the smoke of his cigarette.

"What's on your mind, Stan?" he asked shortly.

Holcomb took his time about putting his full-dress hat down, taking off his white gloves. Then he opened the drawer of the table and lifted out a stack of papers, took a single sheet from the top and flipped it across to Joe. Joe knew what it was.

Each first classman in the company had been directed to submit a statement as to what he considered the essentials of troop leadership to be. Joe had handed his own paper in this morning, beating the deadline by minutes. His views had been terse and to the point — a single sentence scrawled across the paper bearing his name.

You take care of your men.

Holcomb said coldly now: "This paper is unsatisfactory. Do it over. You've got until evening chow to turn a proper paper in to me here. Do you understand?"

"What's wrong with this one, Holcomb?" Joe asked softly.

He saw the familiar flush creep up into Holcomb's face — he was one who couldn't tolerate having his judgment questioned. Joe had found that out long ago. Holcomb picked up the stack that the other papers made and thrust it out angrily.

"Everything's wrong with it!" he snapped. "Everybody but you wrote at least two pages — you wrote one line! I'm responsible that Major Wilson's orders are carried out in this company. If you think I'm going to turn that feeble effort of yours in to him on Monday morning, you've got another think coming! I'm not going to take the rap because you either don't know what leadership means or, if you do know, you're too lazy to put it down!"

"What's wrong with it, Stan?" he said again.

Holcomb grabbed the paper and shook it. His voice was hoarse and angry as he said, "It means nothing! Do it over! It doesn't mean a thing!"

"It means everything," Joe said quietly.

He wheeled and went out, and Holcomb's voice followed him down the hall to his room. "If you haven't turned a new paper in here by evening chow, you'll be reported for direct disobedience of orders. That's final!"

Joe made no answer. Holcomb had his neck stuck out good this time, he decided grimly. He might be company commander, but he had no authority to order Joe to change an official paper and, if he reported Joe for insubordination, it wouldn't be Andrade that got hurt this time. There'd be an investigation and, when the smoke had cleared away, it would be Stan Holcomb who would be doing the bleeding.

So Joe's thoughts ran as he changed into dress gray. It served the guy right, he decided vindictively; but he knew that it was no good. A part of it is your fault, Joe, the back of his mind kept saying. Even if it wasn't, you can't just stand by and watch him cut his own throat to get even.

He remembered what McGraw had said that afternoon, sitting on the bed in the ward as he'd spoken of his father. *A good officer looks after his own.* Joe had never forgotten that. It had inspired the line he'd written on the offending paper. And now he was abandoning his own creed. Nope, it wouldn't wash. Maybe he hated Stan's guts, but you didn't watch a

classmate reaching for a booby-trap and just stand by
while it blew up in his face.

Chubby King came in as Joe was getting his blouse
on. "So what did the great Holcomb want?" Chubby
asked.

Joe shrugged and put on his cap. "He was unhappy
with my leadership paper," he said with a wry grin.
"I am to turn in a new one — at least two pages of
same — before evening chow. That shoots the afternoon. I've got to go tell Sue now."

"Holcomb's got no right to do that, Joe," King said
violently. "Why don't you tell him? Major Wilson
would countermand that order in a minute if he
knew about it."

"Forget it," Joe said, and gave the explanation that
would be the easiest for others to understand. "Just
say that I don't want to gamble an afternoon with Sue
against my last six demerits, Chub. Sue will understand — she and I are going to have a lot of afternoons
together after graduation rolls around."

He went on out and down the stairs, the sound of
his footsteps carrying to the room where Stan Holcomb sat with his mouth tight and angry. After a moment Holcomb got out of his chair and went to the
window that looked down on the area. He watched

Joe crossing to where Sue waited in the sally port; then he returned to his table and deliberately got out a pen and paper. He had written: "Subject: Direct Disobedience of Orders," when King entered the room.

"Writin', Stan?" King asked softly. "I think maybe you'd ought to do a little readin' first. Read on this!"

He slid a stiff sheet across the table's top and Holcomb let it lay, not looking at it as he stared coldly up at King. "I can't think of anything that you could have that I'd care to read, King," he said. "Now get out of here. I'm busy."

"Stole that there out of Joe's desk," King said blandly. "He don't know I know about it, but there ain't much gets by ole Chub King. You read it, boy. It tells why they gave Sergeant Joe Andrade the Silver Star in Korea. Purple Heart goes with it too."

Shocked disbelief suddenly came into Holcomb's eyes as he pulled the paper toward him. The words seemed to dance a little as he read. ". . . for gallantry in action . . . near Woeny'ong-ri, Korea, while a member of Company D . . ." Holcomb finished finally, and all of the starch had gone out of him.

"So he was in Korea," he said slowly. "He fought there. I thought he'd just been in a training camp."

"You've got a lot to learn," King said crisply as he reached for the citation. "Not much time to do it in, either."

It was late afternoon when Joe had finally sweated through his two pages on leadership — written words did not come easy for him. He'd merely repeated his original theme in a dozen different ways, he thought glumly.

Sue had been disappointed at the loss of the afternoon, he knew, but Sue was a good guy. She hadn't griped and he'd make it up to her at the hop tonight. Tomorrow he'd tell her the very special things that he'd meant to say this afternoon.

Joe shrugged the thought away now — gathered up his papers and went down the hall. Stan Holcomb was sitting at his table, looking at Joe's original paper, as Joe slapped his new effort down.

"Two pages!" he said shortly. "You can start tearing up that report for insubordination now, Holcomb!"

Holcomb gestured toward a crumpled wad in front of him. "I already have, Joe," he said in a sober voice. "I guess I've been a pretty big heel. I'm sorry about

your new paper — the first one said all there is to say.
I can see that now."

"Huh?" Joe demanded in a startled voice.

Holcomb met his eyes squarely. "I know about
your Silver Star, Joe," he said slowly. "Why didn't
you just tell me when I told you to rewrite that
paper? You'd have made a dead duck out of me if
you had."

For a moment Joe stared down at the other — then
his homely face broke into its easy grin. "Shucks, I
had to keep you around, pal," he said. "Who'd I have
to stand guard over those last six demerits, if I didn't?
I was just being practical."

Holcomb thought that over — then put out a hand.
"Thanks, Joe," he said quietly. "I've just learned
that gallantry doesn't have to be confined to action.
I'd like to shake hands—if you don't mind shaking
with a fool."

"I'm the hand-shaking type," Joe told him, grinning.

D: